The Very Metal Diary of Cleo Howard

By Sarah Tipper

www.fast-print.net/store.php

The Very Metal Diary Of Cleo Howard
Copyright © Sarah Tipper 2014

All rights reserved

No part of this book may be reproduced in any form by photocopying or any electronic or mechanical means, including information storage or retrieval systems, without permission in writing from both the copyright owner and the publisher of the book.

The right of Sarah Tipper to be identified as the author of this work has been asserted by her in accordance with the Copyright, Designs and Patents Act 1988 and any subsequent amendments thereto.

A catalogue record for this book is available from the British Library

ISBN 978-178456-020-1

First published 2014 by
FASTPRINT PUBLISHING
Peterborough, England.

The Very Metal Diary of Cleo Howard

By Sarah Tipper

Dedication

To Mum with lots of love always.

Acknowledgements

I've hugely enjoyed reading books which are fictional teenage diaries, most notably those by Sue Townsend and Rae Earl (and also, at the other end of the age spectrum, Kensington Gore's Diary). I've loved and repeatedly viewed TV programmes which are retrospectives, for instance Kathy Burke's Walking and Talking and Emma Fryer and Neil Edmond's Home Time. These set my mind whirring backwards with their wonderful observations of both simpler and somehow more complex times, before you'd properly grown into yourself. These books and programmes inspired me to have a go at my own similar backwards looking fictional diary. It's a lot of fun when it's no longer your day to day reality.

I'd like to acknowledge and say a big hello to everyone I knew as a teenager and everyone I went to school with. Sorry for the times I was an idiot and I hope you have all reached a happy place in your lives.

A big thank you to all those who have encouraged me to write and to those who have helped to promote the Eviscerated Panda trilogy: John Rainnie, Kate Dixon, Pat Tipper, Suzi Tipper, Derrine Webb, Gary Webb, Steve Betts, Jason Soper, Alan Stubbs, Kensington Gore, Stjöhn J Töwnsend, Pat Bennett, Brett Scarrott,

Inez Yule, Fiona McAnaney, Jennie Manion, Gio Rocha, Chris Booker, Steven 'Trigger' Swan, Nancy Dias, Joe Samuels, Bex Darch, Emma Edwards, Sharron Milton, Rob 'Biz' Hume, Paul Axtell, Zoë Boreham, Bernie Galewski, John Field, Hannah Boschen, Larry Paterson, Mark Wells, Dan Atkins, Spike Walker, Line Berge Torgrimmsen, Ivor Coffey (he invented the udders gesture that has fictionally become Ian's in this book, see August 2nd), Aliana Jones, Hannah Field, Dan Woodcock, Vicky Lopez, Morgan Einon, Liisa Paloniemi, Heikki Hakkarainen, Joel Wheeler, Sarah Bailey, Alison Taylor, Dave Ewart, John Slaymaker, Jen Cripps, Panda Martyn Minns, Johnny Main, Judith Fisher, www.metaltalk.net, Rachel Lister, Dave Rickett, Tal Fineman, metalheadmedia.co.uk, www.geeksofdoom.com, Dan Bond, www.denimandleatheruk.net, Shane Douthwaite, Jorge Zamudio, www.metal-temple.com, Pete Woods, ww.avenoctum.com, Sergey Truekhan, www.drugmetal.ru, www.sonicabuse.com, Phil Stiles, Jamie Hill, www.theocelot.co.uk, Madeline Cheah, Coventry University Evolve Magazine, Nickie Hobbs, www.devolutionmagazine.co.uk, Miranda Yardley, www.terrorizer.com, Mark Barry for interviewing me for his wonderful blog http://greenwizard62.blogspot.co.uk/,Warehouse Studios for allowing Heavy Metal Panda to visit their control room, Iain Purdie from Moshville Times, Natalie Berry from Mad About Books, Stewart Garden, Oxfordshire Music Scene magazine, Jesse Smith, welovemetal.com, weloveourbooks.com, Di Parkes, metalshockfinland.com, Matt Bacon, www.twoguysmetalreviews.com, www.metalised.net, Deena Rae, e-bookbuilders.com, Ngaire Elder, Susan Helene Gottfried, westofmars.com, all rock fiction authors, anyone who ever drank in the now sadly defunct Gloucester Arms in Oxford, anyone who has ever drunk in the Wheatsheaf in Oxford, anyone who has ever drunk in the Nightlight in Hamburg, facebook likers of the page, twitter followers and many more lovely people I had random chats with.

Introduction

The year is 1997. Cleo Howard is at a very awkward age, she's sure she's an adult, so why won't everyone realise this? Why won't her chest realise this? Why is Maths so hard? When will she stop feeling sad that her Dad doesn't live with her and her Mum? Music and men are her twin fascinations and she thanks Almighty Lemmy for metal and mates. Her diary, which you now hold in your hands, is home to her deepest thoughts, fondest wishes and often what she had for tea.

There is a list of characters in the back of the book should you need it. If you want to read more about Cleo Howard, her later adventures are covered in The Eviscerated Panda Trilogy; Eviscerated Panda A Metal Tale, Eviscerated Panda Back In Bamboo and Eviscerated Panda Vulgar Display Of Panda.

If you want to see pictures of a furry chap called Heavy Metal Panda having fun or find out when new books will be available you can like on facebook at www.facebook.com/EvisceratedPanda or follow on twitter at twitter.com/evisceratedpand

January

Wednesday 1st January 1997
Happy New Year, Dear Diary. You were a present from Aunty Alice who always sends a book of some sort. You have a plain cover so I'm going to customise you and then you can help me record all the amazing stuff that happens to me this year. Big responsibility I know, but I'm also putting my Kerrang! 1997 year planner up on my wall by my bed so you don't have to remember stuff for me, you can just chronicle all the epic adventures I have. Right now my planner looks a bit bare. I am fourteen and ten months old, surely my life should be more exciting by now. I need to sort this out...

I'm eating After Eights at five pm, I'm a chocolate maverick!

Thursday 2nd January
Resolutions:
1. Stop worrying about my boobs. They will grow when they're ready.
2. Try harder at Maths. I know I'm not thick but sometimes in Maths I feel well duncey.
3. Stop being shy around men I like. Talk to people instead of leaving it to Jenni and Ian.
4. Take my mugs and plates downstairs.
5. Stop feeling sad that Dad doesn't live with us.
6. Put my washing in the laundry basket.
7. Clean out Mustaine's bowl regularly.

Friday 3rd January

I just re-read yesterday's entry, Dear Diary, and realised I should point out that Mustaine is my goldfish. I named him because Dave Mustaine is ginger (like me and my goldfish) and because Dave Mustaine is an awesome guitar god who would be welcome in my bedroom any day (Mum would have to be out obviously). Today Jenni and I went into town to look at the sales. We went to HMV, Woolworths, C&A, Heelas and Jacksons. I love Jacksons. It is on Jackson's corner and it's like stepping into "Are You Being Served?" Everything is wooden and old fashioned, even the faces of the sales assistants. There is a haberdashery department and solid old lady bras and no fashionable clothes whatsoever. Jenni and I like to look at the beads in the haberdashery and at the jewellery.

I always expect to see Mrs Slocombe but she must be on a tea break when I go in or attending to her pussy! I did see the lady who sold me my first bra last year. I blushed but I don't think she recognised me (would she have recognised me with my top off Dear Diary? Or did she see me and think there's a 32A? Would you go a bit weird if you saw boobs all day?)

We decided to save our money to spend in the pub. Then we called for Ian. His Dad was out so we watched Spinal Tap. I can't decide if Nigel Tufnel or David St Hubbins is the fittest.

Saturday 4th January

After much reflection I think David St Hubbins is the fittest. I've literally been thinking about this since yesterday so it's not a snap decision. I usually like dark haired men, so I needed to be sure. Tonight at the Green Man (Reading's best pub, Dear Diary) there was me, Ian, Jenni, Bob and Simon The Raspberry. I love going to the pub. We sat in a corner by a fireplace. There was great stuff played on the jukebox: Megadeth's "In My Darkest Hour", Ozzy Osbourne's "Bark at the Moon", Slayer's "Angel of Death" and Entombed's "Demon".

Ian is worried about his Grandad. He is in hospital and is not expected to live for much longer. His Dad and his Nan are going to the hospital to visit every day. Ian is going to see him tomorrow. We tried to take his mind off it by posing important dilemmas like would he rather marry Doro Pesch, Gwen Stefani, Courtney Love, The Great Kat or Lita Ford? He said he'd need to date them all for a bit to decide.

Saturday nights have the potential to be very exciting. Jenni is always secretly hoping we'll see Lex from the sixth form or Darren from the year above. Lex is one letter short of sex and Jenni thinks he's the Goth equivalent of the bee's knees or the dog's bollocks. He's sort of the bat's wings Dear Diary. Also his name sounds like Lux, as in Lux Interior from The Cramps. Darren, while not a Goth, is a very fit metal head, and Jenni calls him Dazzling Darren (in private and in her head, not out loud, that would be weird).

I'm always sort of hoping that we'll see Tyrannosaurus Reg. He's in the year above me and was named Reginald after his Grandad. Everyone calls him Tyrannosaurus Reg or T-Reg because Reg is such an old fashioned name. He's got long brown hair and brown eyes. He's much more likely to go out with Ella or Lizzie than with me though. They are the two metal girls in the year above, both of whom Ian likes. However, he knows he has no chance with older women. He also likes a few girls in our year. His current fave is Natalie West, but she doesn't know it and I'm sworn to secrecy.

The brilliant thing about going to the pub is that we could meet new people that don't even go to our school. The not brilliant thing about the pub is that I'm always too shy to talk to new people.

Sunday 5th January
I realise, Dear Diary, I haven't introduced you to people who were at the pub last night. Ian and Jenni are my best mates at school. Jenni is the only Goth in our year. She's tall and smart and beautiful. Ian is tall and I suppose he's handsome but I don't see him that way. Ian and Jenni keep me sane when Mum is arsey (a long sad story Dear Diary, involving a marriage split). I actually rather like school (except Maths and P.E.) because I get to see my mates. Bob and Simon The Raspberry are metal heads in the year above me at school. It's interesting knowing older people. Last year I didn't know what a blow job was so Bob demonstrated using a banana. I still can't look at a banana without blushing but at least I will never be in the embarrassing situation of actually blowing now I know that this is not what you do. Simon gets his name because he spits a bit when he speaks (only a teeny bit, nothing like the Roy Hattersley Spitting Image puppet) and when he was overexcited once he made a raspberry noise.
I took the Christmas decorations down today. This is always my job. Before Mum and Dad separated me and Dad used to put up and take down the decorations together. Mum used to make mince pies for us when we put them up and bacon sandwiches when we took them down.
One of the tiny shiny red parcel decorations with gold ribbon wrapped round it came unravelled when I was undecorating today. I was fascinated by these pretend presents as a child and I

wondered what was in them. It's a block of polystyrene. That's another one of the mysteries of childhood that turns out to be disappointing, like the day I found out Sylvania is a real place but isn't populated by cute animal families, just normal people or like the day I found out what Dad was hiding on top of the wardrobe (my suspicion was sweets) and it was just some playing cards with pictures of ladies in their bra and pants.

Monday 6th January
Back to school today. I wore the leather biker jacket I got for Christmas. Tyrannosaurus Reg from the year above admired it. He felt my shoulder to see if it was real leather! He touched me for about three whole seconds! I think he got aftershave for Christmas because he smelt really pungent. It was nice but I think your eyes would water if you stood too close to him for long. I could sort of feel it in the back of my throat. I sniffed the shoulder of my jacket at home later but I couldn't smell anything except leather.
Mum doesn't work on Mondays, Dear Diary, so she expects me home unless I have a really good excuse. I sometimes do homework on Mondays but we didn't get any today. I watched my Dusk Til Dawn video. I hope I grow boobs like Santanico Pandemonium.

Tuesday 7th January
Ian came round after school and we ate the last two mince pies and the last of the squirty cream. There are only icky orange creams left in the tin of Roses. Farewell Christmas, you were wonderful while you lasted. I love Christmas so much that I can't

help being sad when it's over. It was better when Mum and Dad were together but it's still mostly brilliant.

Wednesday 8th January
Ian's Grandad Alf died yesterday evening. I asked Ian if he was okay. He said he sort of was and he sort of wasn't. His Grandad had been ill for ages. His Dad said he still has to go to school and after school he has to go straight home.
I walked Ian home today then I went to the library. I prefer the actual library to the school library. There's more choice and people don't draw penises in books from the actual library. I get most of my books from the adult section now (where people are adult enough to have seen penises so don't feel the need to draw them). I've read almost everything from the teenage section. I got desperate once and took out a Sweet Valley High book but it was vomitsome.
Today I took out:
The Outsiders by S.E. Hinton
The Hitch Hiker's Guide to the Galaxy by Douglas Adams
This Other Eden by Ben Elton
Claudine At St Clare's by Enid Blyton
The Mating Season by P.G. Wodehouse

Thursday 9th January
I had tea at Jenni's (but they call it dinner). We had salmon that wasn't out of a tin. Until Jenni came to tea at our house she had never had Butterscotch Angel Delight (and to think people say where she lives is the good end of town! Sometimes for pudding they just have fruit!!) After tea we listened to the Sisters Of Mercy's Vision Thing album in her room and wrote our Gods lists.

These are the men (and sometimes women) who we admire most in the world and who we'll probably date when we leave school or get into the sixth form.

Me:
Glenn Danzig
Peter Steele
Tom Araya
Christopher Lee
Elvira Mistress Of The Dark
Joey DeMaio
Rob Flynn
Max Cavalera
Rob Newman
Dave Mustaine

Jenni:
Peter Steele
Kiefer Sutherland
Nick Cave
Robert Smith
Dave Vanian
Andrew Eldritch
Ingrid Pitt
Johnny Depp
Trent Reznor
Marilyn Manson

Jenni put Doktor Avalanche on her first Gods list but then she found out he was a drum machine, not a real person!

Friday 10th January
When I called for Ian this morning I was all ready to say to his Dad Terry that I was sorry to hear his bad news. I felt sick walking up the path. I hate having to say stuff like this but I know I have to and I am sorry because Terry has already had a sad life, what with his wife (Ian's Mum) having an affair and leaving him. Ian answered the door, Terry wasn't in. He'd gone to see Betty, Ian's Nan, to start arranging the funeral.

I changed at Ian's as usual, Dear Diary. Mum wants me to wear a sensible dull navy jumper and nasty polyester black trousers with a crease down each leg and an elasticated waist to school. This is so unreasonable because our school has no uniform. It's mean of Mum to try and invent one, just because she had to wear one. I get round this by putting my clothes in my school bag (usually a Danzig T-shirt and tight black jeans) and leaving the house dressed in what Mum approves of. I call for Ian every morning before school and change in his bedroom then we walk to school together.

When Mum and Dad split up me and Ian used to joke that we should get his Dad and my Mum together so we could live in the same house and stay up late listening to music. It would never have worked. Terry is too laid back and Mum is too uptight.

In the shop on the way to school I bought Ian a Bounty. It's Alice Cooper's favourite chocolate bar.

Saturday 11th January
I went to the Green Man pub with Ian and Jenni. The way it works Dear Diary, is that we turn up wearing lipstick and smoking and no-one doubts that we're eighteen because we appear to be so

confident. Well, Ian and Jenni appear to be confident, I just follow behind them. Both of them look older than their age because they're tall. We don't draw attention to ourselves and no-one questions us. We don't get too drunk or too noisy so we aren't a nuisance. I've seen people get kicked out for this. It seems to me that you can do what you want so long as you do so discretely, so I don't go boasting about having been to the pub, I just quietly go about my business.

We often see the metal heads from the year above us or the Goths from the sixth form. All the metal/goth/punk people at school sort of talk to each other or at least nod at each other, regardless of what year they are in. It's like an invisible bond. The Green Man is a rock pub so it's full of cool people and has no townies or trendies to bother us. They have their own places, whose door I wouldn't darken for fear of hearing rubbish music. Tonight Bob and Tyrannosaurus Reg were out. Reg is so much hotter than you would think based on his name Dear Diary. I wish I had a photo to show you. I think he's the best looking boy in the year above, but Jenni thinks it's Darren "Dazza" Baskerville.

Sunday 12th January
I just re-read yesterday's entry. I should point out that it's just me and Jenni that wear lipstick to the pub, not Ian.
I lay in bed all morning reading The Hitch-Hikers Guide To The Galaxy and listening to Slayer's Reign in Blood album. Then I got up for dinner (cheese crispy pancakes, peas and mash, followed by yummy Viennetta). Then I lay in bed all afternoon until Mum made me go up the shop for her to get loo roll because we've run out. She made me brush my hair as well as getting dressed! For Lemmy's sake, it's a Sunday, and no-one cares if you buy loo roll

with untidy hair. Also, she works in a supermarket, so why do we keep running out of basic stuff?

Monday 13th January

Today the front page of the Reading Chronicle didn't read "Local People Relieved at Tidy Haired Loo Roll Purchase, Fabric of Society Remains Intact".

Is Textiles the most pointless lesson ever, Dear Diary, or is it P.E.? I started making a pin cushion today in Textiles. This was our first coursework project. I've already done loads of stuff like this with Nanny Howard and with the Brownies so for me it's well easy. Then in P.E. it was raining really heavily so we did loads of games that were basically throwing and catching a ball. Today has contributed nothing to my future career.

I'm wearing naff Christmas novelty socks today with reindeer on because all my other socks are in the wash basket. Dickens said we should keep Christmas in our heart but I'm also keeping it on my feet.

Tuesday 14th January

Ian and Jenni came round after school. Mum was working until eight. We watched my Alice Cooper Welcome To My Nightmare video. They left before Mum got home. Basically Dear Diary we hang out at whoever's house is parent free and if there is no parent free option we either go to town or go to the park, or go to Jenni's. Jenni's house is the biggest and her parents are the least grumpy. Her Dad is a teacher at the University of Reading and he always asks us odd questions. Her Mum is always smiley and doesn't mind Jenni being friends with boys but Jenni has to do all her homework so is often doing this on a Tuesday. Usually

on Tuesday Ian comes to my house after school and Jenni has to do homework. On Wednesday I go to his and Jenni has to do homework, on Thursday I go to Jenni's and we do homework and then are allowed to go up to her room. Ian plays Doom with Matty Bateman most Thursdays. Saturday is always, always pub night. Me, Ian and Jenni have been going since November last year. Before that we used to mainly amuse ourselves in the park, singing and drinking vodka or lovely cherry Lambrini.
Mum bought a slightly squashed lemon meringue pie home with her. Sometimes I love that she works in a supermarket.

Wednesday 15th January
Why do you only get lemon meringue pie? I'd eat apple meringue pie or cherry meringue pie too, but not shepherds meringue pie. I went to WH Smiths on my way home to flick through Kerrang! I didn't bother buying it because Reef are on the cover. I usually buy Kerrang! if there's decent bands in it and Ian always buys Metal Hammer then we swap so we get to read both. Jenni reads them after us and complains that there isn't a special magazine for goths. She sometimes reads her brother Bruce's NME. She also reads her parent's Guardian newspaper most days (yawn) and New Scientist magazine every week. Sometimes I look at the pictures in New Scientist when I'm round her house. Ian and I sometimes read his brother Gav's Viz magazine.
Mum still hasn't done the washing so I'm wearing my Christmas socks with a family of robins in hats on. If they were socks from Switzerland they'd be Swiss family robins on socks! Don't groan Dear Diary, I need to tell jokes to keep myself cheerful. Dad used to tell me jokes all the time but Mum never does, she just sighs

and asks me to make her a cup of tea because her feet hurt. I don't know how tea makes your feet stop hurting.

Thursday 16th January
Talking of feet, Dear Diary, my DMs are finally comfortable. It has taken literally months for them to stop giving me blisters. Mum bought them for me at the start of September last year, ready for going back to school. They are just black eight hole ones. I've been nagging her to get me the cherry red fourteen hole ones, but, even if I get them I'm not sure I could be bothered to wear them in.

Friday 17th January
Ian wasn't at school today because it was his Grandad's funeral. He said he's coming to the pub tomorrow though. Carina Norman was wearing a new denim skirt from Miss Selfridge which does up at the front and is A line (according to Mrs Savage). She was showing off about it in Textiles and saying she still has loads of Miss Selfridge gift vouchers left from Christmas. In Claudine At St Clare's the headmistress tells the girls that they have to judge people on who they are, not what they have but Mrs Savage just said what a complicated pattern it is because it's in sections and has buttonholes and denim is hard to work with. Mrs Savage looks like she buys all her clothes from BHS even though she knows how to make them.
It's a bumper week for squashed cakes. Mum came home with a slightly flattened Black Forest gateau. A new series of Red Dwarf started tonight. I taped it and will take it round to cheer Ian up. Kryten used an attachment in his groinal socket to stir Lister's tea because Lister had swapped Kryten's head and taken out the guilt

chip so they could go back in time for curries. I wish I could take out my shyness chip.

Saturday 18th January

Ian said his Grandad's funeral was horrible. He wore a shirt and tie and his Nan and his Dad were both crying. He hasn't seen his Dad cry since his Mum left. He said afterwards everyone sort of perked up a bit and had some sandwiches in the back room of the pub near his Nan's. His Dad put Elvis's "Always On My Mind" and "Wooden Heart" on the jukebox (and Queen's "Fat Bottomed Girls" because he still had a credit left). Ian's Dad Terry firmly believes that Elvis is alive and well and just got sick of being famous.

Tonight T-Reg, Dazza and Bob were out. The conversation was mostly about music, we always avoid talking about school when we're at the Green Man because a) it's boring and b) we are pretending to be not at school in order to drink there. The best song played on the jukebox tonight was Machine Head's "Davidian". We also heard ZZ Top's "Legs" and we always giggle at the bit where they say "fanny", even though it means bum in America.

Sunday 19th January

Today was access day. Mum and Dad have agreed he can see me every fortnight. There is not much to do in Reading on a Sunday. Some of the shops are open but since Dad moved out both him and Mum have less money. We went to McDonalds and ate chicken nuggets. I'm mostly vegetarian but I don't really like anything in McDonalds except chicken nuggets and I didn't want to be awkward. I wanted to tell him I was sorry about him and

Mum and that I love him but I didn't. The tables are really close together in McDonalds. I could hear chewing from the next table. The toy in the happy meal this week was a Hercules figure. Hercules did twelve really, really hard tasks. It seems a shame to immortalise him in cheap plastic and get ketchup on him.
I finished reading the Hitch Hiker's Guide to the Galaxy. If the meaning of my life is forty-two I hope that's not the age I finally get to snog T-Reg or the age Mum finally stops telling me what to wear.

Monday 20th January
It was so hard to get out of bed today. I wanted to stay in my cosy sleep fog. If it wasn't for Mum shouting up the stairs and for Slayer's "South of Heaven" I'd never have got upright.
Some twats at school today were going on about how great ecstasy is and how Brian Harvey shouldn't have got kicked out of East 17 for taking it. Frankly I don't care how East 17 end, just so long as they do.
Meanwhile, I've got bigger stuff to think about, should I die my hair blonde? The Great Kat looks amazing. Ian said she gives him a stiffy of epic proportions. He thinks she would give the best hand jobs in the world because of her guitar virtuosity. I said maybe she'll tug him off and record his grunting noises and squeals of pleasure as a track on her next album.
Lex and Mopey Dick spoke to me and Jenni today. They are in the sixth form and are Goths. Jenni fancies Lex even more than she fancies Dazza. Mopey needed to borrow some eyeliner. He said he felt naked without it. He talks really slowly, like just being alive is an effort. He sounds a bit like a record played at the wrong speed. His proper name is Richard Rippingdale and he tried to get

everyone to call him "Ripper", which is a very good Goth name, but instead every calls him Mopey Dick, which suits him well. We did long division in Maths today. I did really, really long division because it seems to take me longer than everyone else.

Tuesday 21st January

I started my fifth ever period today. I know last year I was moaning Dear Diary, that I wanted them to start, but now they have I've sort of got a new set of problems. I only wanted them to start as a sign that I'm normal and because I thought my boobs would grow when my periods started.

Annoying things about periods:
1. Have to remember to take a ST with you everywhere
2. Stomach ache and other aches
3. Can get pregnant
4. Mum claims I get moody, which I don't, and it really annoys me when she claims I'm grumpy because of the time of the month.

Wednesday 22nd January

I went round to Ian's after school. Mum is at work until eight. Ian's Dad Terry made us cheese toasties then we sat in Ian's room and listened to Bolt Thrower's In Battle There Is No Law album. I wish I was Jo Bench. I really need to learn how to play bass guitar. Bass guitar plan:
1. Get bass guitar
2. Borrow book on how to play bass guitar from library
3. Practice loads (except Saturdays, pub time is sacred, but Maths homework time can be better spent learning to play bass)

4. World tour with my band, supporting Alice Cooper or Megadeth
5. Rehab
6. Marry Pete Steele after chance meeting somewhere exotic

I won't forget Mum when I'm famous. I'll send her postcards and she'll admit she was wrong to say I couldn't wear my Slayer T-shirt to school. I'll buy her cakes which aren't squashed. I'll invite Dad to come and see me play.

Thursday 23rd January
I nearly got caught smoking behind the Maths block today. Why is everything to do with Maths so much trouble?
I went round Jenni's after school. I did my homework because Jenni always has to sit at the kitchen table and do her homework before we're allowed to go up to her room. When we were upstairs we looked through the Attitude Clothing catalogue and picked the outfits we'd wear if we were double dating T-Reg and Lex.
When I got home I finished reading The Outsiders by S.E. Hinton. It used to be a set text for English but it isn't now. It has a ginger girl in it who is called Cherry and who gets asked if her pubes match her hair. My blood ran cold at the thought of this still being a set text, I'm even glad it's Macbeth this term. Although, the trouble with Shakespeare is that it's all about kings and I don't do History, I do German. The Outsiders was a good book though and more relevant than Shakespeare because in it there were people at their school in America who like all the mainstream stuff (in Reading this is the Spice Girls and Oasis) and then the greasers

who are more interesting (in Reading this is the metal heads, Goths and punks).

Friday 24th January
We had to set fire to a peanut in Biology today. It was to show how much energy is in a peanut. I can tell how much energy is in a peanut by looking at it. Not much, because it's tiny.
Red Dwarf was brilliant tonight. I taped it so I can take the tape round to Ian's tomorrow. Ace Rimmer is back, what a guy! Also they drank cocktails out of pineapples. I hope I get to drink a drink out of a pineapple one day, or a coconut. Ace Rimmer is dying so he has to train Arnold Rimmer to be Ace Rimmer. Ace said there have been lots of Aces, and they all recruit the next Ace before they die. They start off as caterpillars and turn into butterflies.

Saturday 25th January
Me and Ian watched last night's Red Dwarf twice today. Then we called for Jenni and we all went up town. Jenni bought Echo and the Bunnymen's Ocean Rain album because Lex mentioned them on Friday and she doesn't have any of their stuff. She talks to him like he's a normal person and not a) two years older than us, b) one of the fittest males in the entire school. Yesterday she just said "Hi" and asked him what was on his Walkman.
We went straight to the Green Man after we'd been to the shops. Bob and STR were there with Ella and Lizzie. Bob and Ella were sort of flirting and STR and Lizzie weren't. I have never known Lizzie to have a date but Ella has had a couple of boyfriends. Ella said Jon Bon Jovi gives her a special feeling in her lady place. T-Reg also came to the pub tonight. He sat next to Ella, across the

table from me. He accidentally kicked me once but that is as close as I got all evening, Dear Diary. Bob bought some condoms from the machine in the men's loo just in case he got lucky. The only way he would get lucky would be if Ella squinted at him and he sort of looked Bon-Joviesque and ravishable.

Sunday 26th January
I lay in bed listening to Zodiac Mindwarp and the Love Reaction's Tattooed Beat Messiah over and over again. I listened to this all week on the last family holiday me, Mum and Dad went on last year, before they split up. Sometimes when I hear this album I feel like I'm back in the past.
I haven't told you that much about my Dad, Dear Diary. He's called Chas and he is tall, friendly and funny. I've noticed I describe everyone as tall. Maybe this is because I'm not, so everyone else seems to be. Dad used to be the assistant manager of a shoe shop. He said it was a bit like being Al Bundy from "Married With Children" (which was fine by me, because that would make me Kelly, the hot blonde who always dates long haired men). He is now the assistant manager of a jewellers shop but not one that has tons of expensive stuff, which I think is good because it is unlikely to be held up at gunpoint. He is too smart for his job and reads as many books as Jenni's Dad does. He never went to university because Grandad Howard and Nanny Howard couldn't see the point in it. He got married instead (and look how that turned out Dear Diary). I don't know if I will go to university. Dad thinks I should and Mum doesn't mind.
I should probably have done my Maths homework if I want to go to university but I didn't understand it. I do my homework about seventy-five percent of the time. Jenni always does hers because

her Mum asks her every single day if she's got any and it doesn't take her that long anyway because she's so smart.

Monday 27th January
Mrs Butler brought a pile of magazines round for Mum. They are mostly full of nonsense about diets on one page and then fattening recipes on the next page and then a feature on something lame like stencilling an old chest of drawers but I like reading the problem pages in case anyone else is a flat chested sex goddess in waiting and doesn't know what to do to speed this up. I read a few of them but I've just made myself more worried because when you actually start having sex you get a bunch of other stuff to worry about like diseases and pregnancy and if you should get married and what if he's a pervert?

Tuesday 28th January
We made Victoria sponge in Home Ec. Mine turned out great but I've been able to cook this since I was about nine. Most people managed a half decent cake, except Donna Harlow who forgot to put her eggs in.
After school Ian and I went to the chip shop then came back to my house. He stayed until ten minutes before Mum got in from work.
Mum asked me if I'd like my chest of drawers stencilled to brighten my room up a bit. Unless she can do a skull or the Megadeth logo then the answer is no.
Mum thinks all boys are a bad influence, Dear Diary, so I orchestrate it so that she never meets any of my male friends. Ian always leaves before she gets in from work on a Tuesday. He often walks me home from his house on a Wednesday but we

always say goodbye at the lamp post by the massive hedge. Mum thinks all relationships are doomed like her's and Dad's and that you shouldn't have boyfriends until you're eighteen and you shouldn't have sex until you're married and even then it shouldn't be any fun at all.

Wednesday 29th January
Mrs Butler and Mum were talking today in the kitchen about some new people who have just moved into our road. They are called Jean and Josie and Mrs Butler said they have an alternative lifestyle. I asked what sort, hoping they were metal or Goth but Mum said they were like Aunty Elsie. I said "What Welsh?" and she went red and said that they weren't Welsh, they were both ladies and they got on very, very well. She probably meant they were lesbians but she gave me her look which means do not ask any more questions about this right now.
When Mrs Butler went I asked if I could have some Viennetta. Mum said it was for Sunday. I said I was hungry now. I pretended to read the packet and said it didn't say it was only suitable for weekend eating and that we didn't need to stick slavishly to convention now we've got lesbians up the road. Mum said I could have some Viennetta if I shut up and let her have a bit of peace and quiet. I said I was too polite to talk with my mouth full of Viennetta so it was a deal. I asked Mum if she wanted me to cut her a slice of Viennetta and she said "Oh, go on then". I don't know anyone who doesn't like Viennetta, I'd eat it every day if I could.

Thursday 30th January
This morning the Reading Chronicle front page headline didn't read "Woman Eats Viennetta Mid-week, Neighbours Shocked".
I listened to NOFX's "Liza & Louise" and wondered about being a lesbian.

Friday 31st January
I love Fridays. It's Red Dwarf and Mum usually brings us something nice home when she goes shopping. I have to go straight home from school unless I have a good excuse and I have to help put the shopping away. Then I think about what to wear to the pub tomorrow.
Kochanski is back in Red Dwarf tonight and Kryten is jealous of her. Mum bought me a Fuse. These and Spira and Bounty are my favourite chocolate at the moment.

February

Saturday 1st February

I went to Jacksons with Jenni this afternoon. We bought embroidery thread for making friendship bracelets. I got red and black, she got purple and black. Her Mum Pam found us a big safety pin each and we got started. Then we went to the Green Man with Ian. It was just the three of us tonight but still a good laugh.

Sunday 2nd February

Today Dad and I went to see Nanny Howard. She said she'd missed me and gave me a fiver. We watched the telly (Eastenders omnibus) and had some bakewell tart. She gave me a big cuddle when I left and told me I was welcome any time and if I ever need anything I should ask.
When I got home Mum was in a foul mood. She started moaning about all sorts of irrelevant stuff. She said the music I listen to encourages drug taking and Satanism. I showed her the lyrics to Black Sabbath's "After Forever" from Master Of Reality (and put my hand over the lyrics to "Sweet Leaf"). This placated her a bit. I don't think she likes it when I see Dad, the quickest way to get her in a bad mood is to mention him or that side of the family.

Monday 3rd February

Ian and I got soaked today on the way to school. In Textiles Mark Dobbs kept telling me to put my arms out, I thought he was admiring my Alice Cooper T-shirt but actually he was looking at my nipples!! I wasn't wearing a bra today because they are all in the wash basket. Are all boys this revolting? Do all men perve at every opportunity? Even old men in their forties like people's Dads and uncles?

Tuesday 4th February
I'm wearing a bra and a vest today. My nipples are not for public consumption. Me and Jenni both gave Ian a friendship bracelet. You have to make a wish when you tie it on and when it falls off your wish will come true. We made them for each other too, so we've all got two wishes.
Matty Bateman got thrown out of Home Ec. for farting today. He claimed it wasn't him, it was a mouse (it was a squeaky one). Mrs Savage said he wouldn't do that in his kitchen at home. After the lesson Ian said he has heard Matty fart in his kitchen at home, so Mrs Savage is a liar.

Wednesday 5th February
CDT is basically just colouring in. It stands for communication, design and technology and we are meant to get a go on the computers but we never do because the Business Studies class is always using them. Today we were given a sheet of shapes to colour in so that they look 3D. You just have to do darker edges then leave a white bit for where the light would shine.
Kerrang! has Korn and Sepultura this week so is just about worth buying. It also has Redd Kross. I love their Phaseshifter album but all their other stuff is an indie drone I can live without. Terry told us today that we should listen to Queen and Elvis, "You need to acquaint your young ears with rock royalty" he said.

Thursday 6th February
Owen Tranter has been suspended! He bit Jessica Rice on the arse! Dazza was in the Maths class it happened in. It was not long after Mr Kennedy had said that everyone needed to aim for full attendance if they want to get a good grade at GCSE. If Owen fails Maths it will turn out that his biting Jessica on the arse has bitten him in the arse!

I did my English homework and German homework at Jenni's kitchen table. English was just reading a bit of Macbeth and thinking about it. German was a list of words which we had to write the English word next to. I did the German stuff while Jenni read Macbeth out loud so we were done in half the time. One of the German words was Schwarzwälder kirschtorte which I can always remember because it's Black Forest gateau. I hope one day I get to go to Germany and eat an authentic Black Forest gateau. Mum wouldn't let me go on the German exchange trip. She said it was too expensive and it wouldn't be convenient to have a German child stay with us because she has to work three days a week. I was sort of relieved because I don't think I have enough conversational German for it to not be weird. I also wouldn't want to miss going to the pub.

Friday 7th February
Where I sit in Biology is also where Tyrannosaurus Reg sits in Biology. He scratched the Slayer logo into the wooden bench with a compass last year. I like to look at it and know that he's been sat here not paying attention too. Today when I got to Biology some awful pleb had crossed this out and written "Girl Power!" with a permanent marker over the top of it.

What precisely is Girl Power? The Spice Girls are constantly going on about it. It's probably just something they've been told to say by their record company.
Clarity Spices, please.

Saturday 8th February
When I wrote yesterday that where I sit in Biology is also where T-Reg sits in Biology, I should clarify that we have Biology at different times, so I'm not sitting on his lap during Biology although that would be sort of wonderful, but not, because everyone else would also be there.
The Green Man was amazing tonight. T-Reg, Bob, Simon The Raspberry and Sadie were there. Bob was saying how much he likes a weekend to be full of booze and birds. He is rumoured to have had sex with Ella. I know Simon The Raspberry hasn't because everyone teases him about it. I don't know about T-Reg or Sadie. STR follows Sadie around like he's a lost lamb. She is the only punk in the entire school. She has punk mates but they don't go to our school. She was wearing a black leather skirt, fishnet tights with holes in and an Amebix T-shirt. She has a medium sized chest. No-one else had heard of Amebix. She said she has Amebix for breakfast like most people have Weetabix. I usually listen to Slayer and have Coco Pops if there is time (rarely) or a Bounty on the way to school. She put X-Ray Spex's "Oh Bondage Up Yours!", L7's "Shove" and Lunachicks' "Down At The Pub" on the jukebox. She told us to call her "Shot" which is her nickname. Her surname is Gunn. I wish I had a cooler name than Howard. When people hear Howard they think of Howard The Gerbil from The Roland Rat Show, or Howard and Hilda from Ever Decreasing Circles or Howard from Last Of The Summer Wine.

T-Reg was being really filthy and he did the tongue between two fingers "oral sex on a lady" gesture. He claims to have two girlfriends. Sadie, sorry, Shot said "Yeah, your right hand and your left hand" and then he shut up.

Sunday 9th February
I had a big lie in. I wonder if T-Reg does have two girlfriends? He claims neither of them live nearby and this is why no-one has seen them. If he's already got two girlfriends he won't want a third. I've got the Coco Pops jingle stuck in my head and I'm trying to blast it out with Nine Inch Nails's Pretty Hate Machine.

Monday 10th February
For a Monday today has been very acceptable. School was good. I never really mind school except for getting up early, P.E., Maths and when Carina Norman is acting up. Today Carina Norman wasn't there (she is the class bitch, Dear Diary, a total and utter nasty piece of work, as Nanny Howard would say), we did some aerobics in P.E. with a supply teacher and Maths was about angles which I can understand. Ian made me a mix tape. I saw T-Reg in shorts. I made macaroni cheese for tea and it was the best I've ever made, with a really smooth cheese sauce. Mum had some when she got in from work and said it was perfect.
My mix tape from Ian:
Side One:
She-Wolf – Megadeth
Where Next To Conquer – Bolt-Thrower
This Maniac's In Love With You – Alice Cooper
Lady Lust – Venom
Beethoven On Speed – The Great Kat

Die By The Sword – Slayer
L.O.V.E. Machine - WASP
All Men Play On 10 – Manowar
Hammerhead – Flotsam and Jetsam
Sacrifice – Motörhead
Alcohol – Gang Green
Social Sterility – Napalm Death

Side Two:
The Metallian – Iron Angel
You're My Temptation – Alice Cooper
Shoot From The Hip – WASP
Bleed For Me - Dismember
Temptation - Slayer
My Own Worst Enemy – Napalm Death
Voices Carry – Gang Green
Live Like An Angel – Venom
Pleasure Slave – Manowar
Refuse/Resist – Sepultura
Legs – ZZ Top
Beer Drinkers And Hellraisers – Motörhead

There's a bit in L.O.V.E Machine where it sounds like Blackie Lawless is singing "My dick runs through my fingers"! But actually it's "magic runs through my fingers". I like Venom and without them we wouldn't have Slayer but a lot of their stuff sounds like it's been recorded in a cupboard in a hurry.

Tuesday 11th February

Owen Tranter is no longer suspended. He's going out with Jessica Rice. I hope they get married and tell their grandchildren how they met and fell in love.

Donna's tampon fell out of her bag today. I put my foot over it and kicked it over to her discretely. She's always alright to me and I knew if Carina Norman saw it she'd make a massive fuss and shout "You've dropped something Donna" so that everyone would look round.

I have a lot of the same lessons as Ian and Jenni but we usually get split up or made to sit alphabetically. Donna's surname is Harlow so I end up next to her in German and a few other lessons. She likes rap and hip hop but that's preferable to the Spice Girls or Oasis. She has snogged quite a few boys already. Today is pancake day. I hope by next pancake day my chest isn't flat.

Wednesday 12th February

I went round Ian's and we listened to Slayer's Show No Mercy album. I think "Die By The Sword" is my fave track but maybe that's just because it's familiar from my mix tape. It's so exciting. It's enough to distract you from your homework.

T-Reg, Bob and Simon The Raspberry were discussing the girls at our school with Ian. Ian said they said that me and Jenni are two of the fittest girls in our year, but I'm a bit too quiet and Jenni is a bit too posh. I wish Jenni and I could each swap a bit, so she was a bit less posh and I was a bit less quiet. Also, Bob has done it with Ella.

Kerrang! is brilliant this week. There is a picture of Pete Steele in a vest. I'm going to need a cold shower, then another cold shower. He's given me a special feeling in my lady place.

Thursday 13th February

School was brilliant today. There is some building work being done at the sports centre (Dear School Governors, why don't you spend your money on something better, which we actually want, like more computers?) and as I was walking to Maths (with the unhurried stride of someone who doesn't mind arriving late) I saw a long haired builder wearing an Exodus T-shirt! After Maths Jenni and I walked back past again slowly and she pretended to drop her bag (she is so brave and smart, I'd never think of that, or even if I did I wouldn't dare do it). He looked up and smiled at us! He's got one continuous bushy dark eyebrow but I don't care, I still would.

I went to Jenni's after school. We had no homework so went straight upstairs. Jenni has a cooler bedroom than me. For a start it's bigger. It's also painted black and purple. Mine is covered in posters but the wallpaper underneath has clouds and rainbows on (I chose it ages ago when I was obsessed with Care Bears). In Jenni's room there is a Barbie dressed in black PVC hanging from the ceiling (a practice go at a school textiles project that she got forced to change by Mrs Savage), a skull candle and she has a lava lamp (which her parents bought years and years ago).

But, the main way Jenni's room is cooler than mine is that she is allowed to have men in her room! She walked home with Dazza yesterday and he wanted to borrow a Cradle Of Filth CD and her Mum didn't mind him going upstairs to get it! She's had Dazza actually sat on her actual bed! The only males to have seen the inside of my room are Dad and Ian (and Ian wasn't actually allowed. It's just that when Mum's out I'm unbollockable). Jenni's bedroom is practically a boudoir.

Friday 14th February
I got a card! An actual Valentine's card (definitely not from anyone in my family being nice, it came in the post and I found it before Mum, who doesn't believe in love any way). Before you get too excited though Dear Diary, my name was spelt wrong. The card was addressed to Cloe Howard. Whoever it is can't be an intellectual fireball, but maybe they are really fit or they've got a motorbike, in which case it won't matter.
Ian also got a card. He hopes it was from Natalie West but she claimed to have sent no cards. I think it was probably from Charmaine Payne. She looks at him like he's a Malibu and Diet Coke with a cherry and an umbrella in it.
Red Dwarf was really funny tonight. Kryten made The Arnold Rimmer Experience because they were all missing Rimmer since he's gone off to be the new Ace Rimmer.

Saturday 15th February
Mum bought me some half price heart shaped chocolates from the shop she "works" in. I say "works" because every time I've seen her at work she's packing people's shopping and chattering. This gossip while you work arrangement has got me into trouble in the past. I've been reported by acquaintances of Mum's for not wearing my bobble hat in winter and for smoking.
Tyrannosaurus Reg and Simon The Raspberry were at the Green Man briefly tonight but it was a bittersweet meeting because they left to go and meet some girls. I can smell Reg for at least half an hour after he's left. If he ever came round my house I'd need to squirt the Mr Sheen about to mask his manly musky scent before Mum got in. I'm glad I've already got this planned

for future use. I wish the Valentine's card was from him but I'm sure it's not. I'm sadly a year too young for him to notice.

Sunday 16th February
I went to see Nanny Howard with Dad. She had made us trifle. She let me sprinkle the hundreds and thousands on top. Also, she found my pom-pom makers. These are circles of plastic that you put together then wrap wool around, making a sort of doughnut until the middle eventually vanishes, then you cut through all the wool round the circumference (see, I do know Maths words) and then tie a strand of wool round the middle and remove the plastic circles. I used to love these but that was five years ago. I've brought them home with me so as not to offend her. She gave me some wool to go with them.

Monday 17th February
I've had a terrible day at school. At morning break T-Reg said that all ginger girls have really strawberry pink nipples and asked me if he could he have a look at mine to check. I went bright red.
Then in Maths (horrible lesson anyway) Carina the class bitch asked me if I spray my jeans on and said she can't see a pant line so I can't have any knickers on. Jenni gave her a look and she shut up.
After school I went to see Nanny Brooks with Mum. It's Nanny's birthday. We took her a box of Milk Tray and a card with a yellow rose on it. I chose the card. Nanny used to tell me that yellow roses mean love and red roses mean lust! I was only about ten when she told me that. Even then her memory was a bit sketchy and she wasn't always sure who she was talking to.

Today was sad. Nanny didn't know it was her birthday, even though she'd had cards in the post and the warden of the sheltered housing had made her a cake. Sheltered housing is a bit like an Enid Blyton boarding school for old people. Every day they can do things together like bingo or watch telly in the day room. It's quite hard to chat to Nanny. Mum usually talks to her about things from decades ago. It's weird how she can remember a telly advert from the seventies but can't remember her own birthday. Today she could remember the Milk Tray man.

I've finished making a mix tape for Ian:
Side One:
The Hunt - Sepultura
How Will I Laugh Tomorrow - Suicidal Tendencies
Love Gun – Entombed
Burning Inside - Ministry
Pull The Plug - Death
Devil's Plaything - Danzig
She – The Misfits
Let's Break The Law – Zodiac Mindwarp and the Love Reaction
Male Supremacy – Carnivore
Evil Woman – Black Sabbath
I'm Broken – Pantera
In My Darkest Hour - Megadeth

Side Two:
War Inside My Head – Suicidal Tendencies
I Like It Hot – Wolfsbane
The Hunter - Danzig
More Human Than Human - White Zombie

Sanctified - Nine Inch Nails
I Am The Law - Anthrax
The Offspring – Self Esteem
Angelfuck – The Misfits
Walk – Pantera
Set My Criminal Free – Zodiac Mindwarp and the Love Reaction
Predator - Carnivore

Tuesday 18th February
I still don't know who my Valentine's card was from. Ian said maybe the sender spelt my name wrong on purpose to throw me off the scent, but that sounds daft. We walked past the sports centre today and the long haired builder was there again. Jenni stopped to tie her shoelace (not even undone!) and he said "Morning ladies" to us! Ian got in a bit of a huff because of being included in the "Morning ladies". This does happen if people see him from behind. His long hair is gorgeous and just a touch womanly.
I made a massive lasagne in Home Ec. All the recipes we do are for a family of four. Not many people in my class actually live in a family of four. We need broken Home Ec.
We got some post addressed to Josie Ashton at number 96. She is one of the women I thought was Welsh but is actually lesbian. I took it round and put it in her box then I giggled all the way back to our house.

Wednesday 19th February
I had a very weird day at school today. It was my turn to be on reception duty. This, Dear Diary, is a sort of slave labour scheme where you miss a whole day of lessons (brilliant) but you have to

sit outside Mr Murray's office and run errands (not so brilliant). It's like you're the headmaster's servant for the day. If he wants he can call you in to fan him with a big book or to peel grapes for him or he can use you as a footstool or make you ring up his enemies and then quickly call them a wanker before slamming the phone down.

You're meant to read while you're not doing errands but I mostly stared out of the window. I got a couple of good errands, taking a message to the sports centre (past the long haired builder but he was absorbed in mixing some cement) and I had to take a trolley of tea and biscuits to and then from a meeting and the school secretary Mrs Nicholson, let me have a biscuit. But I also had to go and get Owen Tranter, who is the hardest kid in the school out of his class and escort him to Mr Murray's office, where he was probably going to get a detention. Mr Murray wasn't ready for him so he had to stay in reception with me. I remained seated (he has a reputation for biting and I didn't want to make any sudden movements). He spent ages kicking the skirting board while glaring. He is mates with T-Reg so he doesn't tend to bother us metal people much but he is feared throughout the school.

Thursday 20th February
Mum asked me today what I want for my birthday. I said vodka, Malibu, a Type O Negative T-shirt, a black leather skirt, my tongue pierced, a tattoo, a bass guitar and loads of CDs. She said I could have a T-shirt and CDs but the other stuff I'll have to wait until I've left school for. She said a bass guitar was too expensive right now but if I still want one at Christmas I might be lucky. What I really want: all of the above plus the issue of Playgirl with Pete Steele in (he's nude, Dear Diary!), a snog with someone (or

everyone!) on my Gods list, Dad to move back in, bigger boobs and to become good at Maths.
If Matty Bateman asks you to pull his finger Dear Diary, don't do it. I only really talk to him because he and Ian are mates. He's very childish and only interested in his computer.

Friday 21st February
I've updated my Gods list just in case the cosmic forces of the universe are aligning to provide me with yesterday's wish for a snog:
Jeff Hanneman – I don't usually fancy blond blokes but he's an exception
David St Hubbins
Zodiac Mindwarp
Glenn Danzig
Santanico Pandemonium
Pete Steele
Dave Lister
Joey DeMaio
Rob Newman
Sean Yseult
If I get to snog any of the above then I'm renaming this month Fabruary.
I think my taste in men is maturing, I'm not so narrow minded that I only fancy men with dark hair any longer.
Red Dwarf was on tonight. They went to Pride and Prejudice world. I tried to read Pride and Prejudice once but it was boring. It was just about getting married which I'm not sure I want to do. Also, Mr Darcy reminds me of Mopey Dick, who is sort of grouchy when you try and be friendly to him.

Saturday 22nd February
Jenni asked what I thought about Dolly today. At first I thought she'd gone wrong in the head and was referring to Dolly Parton but it's actually a cloned sheep called Dolly. I'm glad I'm good at English because Science leaves me a bit baffled. It seems that they've basically made a sheep using only one sheep, not two. Anyway, something even better happened today. I was looking at the pub jukebox and the barman called me over. I was worried he was going to ask me for ID but he gave me three free songs! He didn't have long hair but he was still quite cute. I chose Megadeth's "Sweating Bullets" for Ian, Sisters of Mercy's "More" for Jenni and Type O Negative's "Love You To Death" for me. Then I worried that the barman would think that my songs were a secret coded message to him, which they weren't. Then T-Reg, Darren, Shot and Ella came in.
T-Reg was trying out his chat up lines in the pub. These are his best ones:
Do you like camping?
Because you've made me erect a tent in my pants!
Did you know you've got eyes like spanners?
They make my nuts tighten!
Is there a mirror in your knickers?
Because I can see myself in them!

I've never spoken much to Ella but she seems okay, I'd like to ask her what it was like doing it with Bob. Me and Jenni told her about our Gods lists. Ella fancies Sebastian Bach (Fair enough), Steven Tyler (scarily large mouth but probably a brilliant shag because he's quite old so he's done it loads), Vince Neil (I'm a Tommy Lee or Nikki Sixx girl) and of course Jon Bon Jovi (urrgh!).

Sunday 23rd February
I had a massive lie in and thought about chat up lines. I don't have any. Also, even if I had some, I suspect I'd struggle to use them.
Potential chat up lines:
Hello Pen, fancy a shag? (Okay, I've nicked this from Edward Hitler of Bottom fame but I have to start somewhere).
Would you like a worm do? (Okay, I've nicked this from Rimmer).
Nice T-shirt, it'd look even better on my bedroom floor (but I'm not allowed boys in my room so this is unusable).
I also thought about science. If I was a scientist I'd investigate how to get a chest like Dolly Parton's and leave creating sheep from only one sheep right to the end of my to do list. Sheep seem to have got making more sheep sorted without our human intervention. Also, Mum says lamb is fatty so we don't have it. Plus I could live without knitwear. I'd just wear a long sleeved T-shirt under my usual T-shirt in winter.

Monday 24th February
Half term. It snowed a bit today. Bloody typical. Also I got my period. Bloody typical! At least I got it when I was at home and near some sanitary towels. I hate those words. Mum can't even say it. She says "Do you need some more STs when I go shopping?" I do need some more STs, I don't have all their albums.

Tuesday 25th February
We ran out of cheese so I made marmite and spaghetti hoop toasted sandwiches. They were amazing, well, the second round were. Don't over fill them or the bread won't toast.
Dilemma for Ian: would you rather have the guitar talent of Dave Mustaine or the long tongue of Gene Simmons? He answered instantly the guitar talent of Dave.

Wednesday 26th February
I spent all day at Jenni's. Brie is quite nice except the white bit at the edge but it turns out you aren't meant to eat that bit anyway. We watched The Lost Boys and Edward Scissorhands.
Jenni doesn't intend to lose it until she has been with someone for at least six months. She wants something special she says, not some hurried fumble while someone's parents are out or worse still in the park. Bruce's girlfriend Minty is allowed to stay over in Bruce's room, but they are nineteen and have been together for ages.
It sounds like Jenni is expecting choirs of angels and clouds parting to reveal shafts of sunlight to be attendant on her first shag. Also, she says there's a lot you can do without having actual sex, although she hasn't done any of it yet.
Ian spends a lot of time playing Doom with Matty which along with music seems to fascinate him more than sex, although if Natalie West was an option he'd be up there faster than a Great Kat solo.
I find some men totally fascinating, the way they smell, the way they move, such coiled power in the trouser snake, ready to strike, but is it venom or a love potion?
Dilemma from Jenni: if I was alone with T-Reg for one night and

no one would ever find out what we did and if we had condoms would I do it with him?
I just don't know. Until I was really there I can't say.

Thursday 27th February
Today is my fifteenth birthday. I've had a brilliant day. Mum bought me a massive Body Shop vanilla gift set, a small bottle of vodka, a Type O Negative T-shirt and she gave me vouchers for HMV because she said she didn't want to buy the wrong CDs. She also got me a chocolate cake. Ian gave me a red leather studded belt and Jenni gave me a Nine Inch Nails vest top. I'm going to wear both to the pub on Saturday. I have such awesome friends.

Friday 28th February
Dad took me and Nanny Howard for tea in TGI Fridays. I think it must be hard for them to recreate an American diner near a busy roundabout on a retail park in Reading. There were lots of toddlers running about being noisy, much to Nanny Howard's disgust. She had a burger but she ate it with a knife and fork. I don't think she was impressed. Dad had steak.
There was a letter missing from the words in chrome around the bar so it read "Good imes" rather than "Good times". It was a bit shabby. There was a nice picture of The Fonz and some of the music wasn't too terrible but there was some Springsteen.
Dad bought me a chunky silver chain necklace with a star on it. Nan gave me a matching bracelet. I put both on straight away. I had a burger (which I ate like a normal person) and an ice cream sundae. It's always nice to see Dad but then sad when he goes to his bedsit and I go home, which used to be his home too. I can't say the things I want to say to him when we're surrounded by

people. I've never seen his bedsit. I think it's probably really crappy and he's protecting me from it. He could live with Nanny Howard if he wanted but I don't think he does. Why does no one in my family get on properly? Mum makes us all pretend to in front of other people but it's just a big act. Sometimes I'd like to go back to the sixties when people loved each other and there wasn't AIDS. The only downside would be the lack of decent music.

March

Saturday 1st March

The Green Man was ace tonight. T-Reg, Shot, Bob, Lex and Mopey Dick were out. Everyone wished me happy birthday. Ian bought me a Malibu and Diet Coke. I had to pretend it was my nineteenth birthday. T-Reg gave me a kiss on the cheek! Shot said she'd make me a mix tape if I wanted. I said yes please. Mopey Dick said birthdays just bring you one year closer to death. Then he moaned because you can't buy absinthe in the pub and so he had to make do with snakebite and black. Jenni sat next to Lex and was asking him about where he wants to go to university. The trouble with fancying someone in the sixth form is that they will be leaving after A Levels.

Me and Ian walked Jenni home. Then Ian walked me home and we hugged goodnight at the hedge we always hug goodnight at. He kept not letting me go and giving me extra birthday hugs.

Sunday 2nd March

I listened to Ozzy Osbourne's "I Just Want You" a load of times today. I thought about T-Reg a bit, but mostly I thought about Danzig. One of the things I like about Danzig is that he's not too tall so you would be able to snog him easily if you were standing up. He is five foot three, the exact same height as me.

I finished reading Ben Elton's This Other Eden. The bit where Jurgen Thor and Rosalie have sex is beautiful but not informative.

Monday 3rd March

The phone bill has come. Most people I know get bollocked when the phone bill comes but I hardly use it. We only got it when Dad moved out. It makes me sad to talk to him on the phone so I don't even phone him often.

Tuesday 4th March
Today I'm only talking to you and to my goldfish Mustaine, Dear Diary. It's the only way to get any sense in this house. Mum has just asked when I'm going to grow out of wearing black T-shirts and start wearing nice clothes. She has offered to take me shopping. No, thank you very much, I'll not be troubling the racks of BHS and QS and the other sucky places you like to get clothes from. She has claimed I won't get a husband looking like this. Well maybe I don't want a husband, maybe women in the nineties have more to aspire to (I don't know what yet, but that's just a detail). Also, one minute she doesn't want me to grow up and treats me like a child and the next minute she's banging on about husbands.
Also, Carina Norman asked me today if I was a Satanist. The world has gone mental. She asked if it was sacrificed goat mince in my spaghetti Bolognese in Home Ec. Then everyone stopped listening to her because Donna Harlow got told off by Mrs Rogers for not browning her mince properly.

Wednesday 5th March
Lex made Jenni a mix tape, she is well chuffed. I think a lot of the songs are the sort of songs you would play to someone you fancy. This is what he put on it:
Side One:
Where The Wild Roses Grow – Nick Cave and the Bad Seeds and Kylie Minogue
I Just Can't Be Happy Today – The Damned

Close To You – The Cure
Set Me On Fire – Type O Negative
Pleasure In Restraint – Genitorturers
For My Fallen Angel – My Dying Bride
I Wanna Get In Your Pants – The Cramps
Track X – Sheep On Drugs
Burn – Sister Machine Gun
I Walk The Line – Alien Sex Fiend
Spooky – Lydia Lunch

Side Two:
Beautiful People - Marilyn Manson
Love Will Tear Us Apart – Joy Division
Nocturnal Me – Echo and the Bunnymen
Please, Please, Please Let Me Get What I Want - The Smiths
Your Best Nightmare – London After Midnight
Weak - Skunk Anansie
Torch – Sisters Of Mercy
Darkly Erotic – Cradle Of Filth
Be My Druidess – Type O Negative
Have Love Will Travel - Crazyhead
Deliverance – The Mission

I think if she wanted to Jenni could snog Lex. I remembered today that I never found out who sent me a Valentine's card. I probably won't now. It's just my luck to have a shy admirer, although if it is someone I don't fancy it's easier to not find out and not have to let anyone down.

Thursday 6th March

Charmaine Payne was asking me loads of questions about Ian today. I think she fancies him but I didn't ask her outright. Speaking impartially Dear Diary, he's above average looking, but I couldn't fancy him because I know him too well. Some of the girls in our year are put off by his long hair but some of them think it makes him more exciting. About once a week me and Ian get accused of being boyfriend and girlfriend because we spend a load of time together. We aren't and we never will be, but we will always be friends.

I love "Hammerhead" by Flotsam and Jetsam but I'm not sure I'd pick the Hammerhead shark to compare my penis to if I had one, it's just the wrong shape. Plus there's another bit of the song that puzzles me:

"Come forth and take me, she talks with her eyes".

How do you talk with your eyes? Is it easier than talking with your mouth? If so I'll give it a go.

Friday 7th March

Dilemma for Ian: would you rather be wanked off by Natalie West for twenty minutes or have actual sex with her for five minutes? Ian picked actual sex for five minutes. He claimed she'd think he was so good at it she'd beg him to continue. Confidence in a man is very attractive.

Saturday 8th March

I spent my birthday money on a pink rubber skirt from a shop in the Harris Arcade. Mum went mental. I don't see what the problem is, it's my money! Just because she wants to dress like

she's a colour blind nun from the nineteen fifties doesn't mean I have to. She said it's too short. I said it isn't.
Salvation came in the form of Mrs Butler popping round with some spare onions from her vegetable patch which distracted Mum for long enough for me to get dressed to go to the pub (pink rubber skirt, black tights, Nine Inch Nails vest). I said goodbye to Mum from mostly behind the door. She was watching Noel's House Party.
If I get invited to Noel's House Party (unlikely I know, Dear Diary) I won't go. I bet Mum would though. Why is Mr Blobby capable of making anyone over thirty laugh hysterically?
Everyone in the Green Man admired my skirt. T-Reg said it's wipe clean ability would be good if I ever got jizz on it. Shot said I look cute in pink and sweet like bubble gum. She's always lovely. Ella said my skirt was the same colour as her bra and she flashed it at me. All the men went quiet. STR said he was putting the image of Ella's bra in his wank bank. A wank bank, Dear Diary, is a database of images men keep to help them reach a satisfactory conclusion when pleasing themselves. Bob said he's got a bit of all the women he's met in his. On the way home Ian said my new skirt is a wank bank worthy image.
I realised my skirt is the same colour as Mr Blobby. So far it's not got any jizz on it.

Sunday 9th March
Today is Mother's day. I got Mum a three pack of Walnut Whips from Woolworths and I made her a cup of tea. We went to visit Nanny Brooks in her sheltered accommodation. Mum took her some daffodils but she couldn't find a vase so she put them in an

old brown Smarties mug that once held an Easter egg. Nanny Howard has a crystal vase.
I finished reading The Mating Season by P.G. Wodehouse. It had no rude bits (I borrowed it based on the title) but it was very good. Wooster's aunts sound like their mission is to stop him from having any fun and I know what that's like.

Monday 10th March
Today is Ian's birthday. I bought him Sepultura's Roots album on CD. He was well chuffed. Jenni bought him a Megadeth Peace Sells T-shirt. His Dad got him an acoustic guitar and said he can have an electric one at Christmas if he still wants one. Usually Terry is spot on and fairly sensible (apart from firmly believing that Elvis is alive and that Queen are the best band ever) but he's held back Ian's musical career with a guitar you can't plug in.
Some girls from our year, including Carina Norman, tried to get into RG1 s on Saturday but failed. Haha! That's what you get for wanting to listen to rubbish chart music. Carina glared at Jenni today when she said the bouncers there do a very worthwhile job, keeping the riff raff out.
Charmaine Payne said she'd give Ian a birthday kiss but I think he thought she was joking because he didn't do anything about it.

Tuesday 11th March
Sports Centre Over Blessed Eyebrow Builder spoke to me again today (I must find out his name Dear Diary, I bet it's something exotic and wonderful). He asked me if I had a light. While I was fumbling in my bag he asked me if I like metal. I said yes. Then he asked me who my favourite band is. My mind went totally and utterly blank for about five seconds. Then I mumbled "Slayer"

even though I don't really have one favourite band. He lit his cigarette and his hand sort of touched mine when he gave me back my lighter. He said he'd seen Slayer in London last year, at Brixton Academy and they were spectacular. He looked a bit dusty and I thought about him in the bath.

Wednesday 12th March
When I wrote yesterday that I thought about him in the bath, Dear Diary, I meant that I wondered what Eyebrow Builder would look like naked, not that I had a bath and while doing so I thought about him.
Robb Flynn is on the cover of Kerrang! this week. Yes, Kerrang! magazine you may have my money.
The metal builder with the eyebrow is called Barry. I heard one of the other builders shout it and he answered. This is not a sexy name. The test is to see if you can imagine yourself saying it at the height of passion and if it sounds good it's a sexy name. I can't imagine saying "Do it to me, Barry" without giggling. His eyebrow looked really massive today and I noticed that he has really hairy arms.

Thursday 13th March
I went to the library after school. I've read everything we've got in the house except Mum's Barbara Taylor Bradford collection and Brave New World by Aldous Huxley which looks okay but we aren't doing it until next term so I don't want to read it before I have to.
I took out five books:
Forever by Judy Blume because apparently there is a rude bit, so it's never available in the school library.

Soul Music by Terry Pratchett.

An Introduction To Psychology by Nicky Hayes and Sue Orrell (so I can learn to be less weird around men I like, learn to read minds and learn how to make Mum let me wear what I want).

The Secret Diary Of Adrian Mole Aged 13 and ¾ by Sue Townsend.

Z For Zacariah by Robert C. O'Brien.

Jenni came with me but didn't take any books out. She looked up ejaculation. According to Masters and Johnson the usual distance of an ejaculation is 30 to 60 cm and the usual volume is between 0.1 and 10 millilitres (so a maximum of two teaspoons). Jenni pointed out that if we were to time an ejaculation and measure the distance it travelled, we could work out it's speed. I pointed out that we are very unlikely to be asked to do this in Physics, unless we get a really pervy supply teacher.

Friday 14th March

Mega brilliant day today. Ian and I had a Bounty for breakfast. I wonder if Alice Cooper likes the milk chocolate or the dark chocolate one best? I like the milk chocolate one. At break time we were all hanging around behind the Maths block as usual. T-Reg pinged my bra strap. I pretended I was annoyed but actually I'm well chuffed because:

   a) I have a bra to ping
   b) T-Reg knows I have a bra to ping
   c) T-Reg is looking very cute right now. His hair has got really long and he has an almost complete moustache. I would give anything to feel the tickle of that moustache on my face Dear Diary, even submit to a full hour of bra strap pinging.

Saturday 15th March

Last night I dreamt that Barry was a wolf and he was going to huff and puff and blow my pants down. I woke up before he did sadly. He is so hairy he could be an extra in the Bark At The Moon video. You could probably use him to dry yourself off after a bath.

Shot gave me a mix tape tonight at the Green Man. She's shaved the sides of her head and is wearing loads of black eye make-up. She looks old enough to drink in the pub and she looks hard but she's always really sweet to me. I think Simon The Raspberry is in love with her. He watches her a lot and always lets her choose a song when he puts stuff on the jukebox. Ella and Lizzie were really giggly tonight. They had been drinking Peach Archers (yum) before they came to the pub. They put Van Halen's "Why Can't This be Love", Bon Jovi's "You Give Love A Bad Name" (I wouldn't inflict this on my friends) and Aerosmith's "Walk This Way" on the jukebox.

Sunday 16th March

I had a lie in. I wondered if hairy men are better in bed because they have more testosterone?

Dad took me to see Nanny Howard. This is becoming what we do every access Sunday now.

When I got home I listened to the mix tape Shot made me. I love it. I'm going to make her a friendship bracelet.

Side One:
Oh Bondage Up Yours! – X Ray Spex
Woman – Anti Nowhere League
Dying World – Sub-Humans

You – Bad Religion
Six Pack – Black Flag
Roads To Freedom – Cock Sparrer
Bubble Gum – All
Gonna Find You – Operation Ivy
Porno Slut – The Exploited
Wild In The Streets – Circle Jerks
Everybody Is On Sale – Alice Donut
Sheena Is A Punk Rocker – The Ramones
Time Bomb - Rancid
Your Emotions – Dead Kennedys

Side Two:
Nothing I Can Do - Sub-Humans
I Don't Wanna Hear It – Minor Threat
Identity – X Ray Spex
Sunday Stripper – Cock Sparrer
Bruise Violet – Babes In Toyland
Orgasm Addict – Buzzcocks
No Values – Black Flag
Punish Me – Poison Idea
Am I Punk Yet? – Electro Hippies
Doesn't Make It All Right – Stiff Little Fingers
The Wars End - Rancid
Stranglehold – UK Subs
Don't Look In The Freezer – Dr and the Crippens

Monday 17th March
Today Barry was wearing a Motörhead T-shirt and he gave me the most amazing smile and said "Good morning Red". I'm

getting used to the name Barry. I remembered that the lead guitarist in Bolt-Thrower is called Barry Thompson, so actually it's a brilliant name.

I read the cartoons in Mum's Daily Express. Why does Garfield hate Mondays? He doesn't go to work or school. Maybe he misses Jon while he's at work or maybe Odie really winds him up when Jon isn't around. Garfield probably wants to sleep but Odie wants to do stuff.

Tuesday 18th March

Dilemma for Jenni: would she rather have her nose pierced or have a 30 second snog with Lex?

I finished reading Judy Blume's Forever. Katherine (whose surname is Danziger – very cool) loses her virginity to Michael who calls his penis Ralph. I think it's weird to name your penis. This was a much realer sex scene than when Rosalie and Jurgen Thor do it, but I'd rather be Rosalie than Katherine. Learning from books just isn't as good as actually really doing things (the Brownie Guide Handbook suggests you practice swimming by lying across a chair and I did this before I learnt to swim but when I was actually in water it was totally different). Dad once went to Oxford on a training course and he bought me back a bookmark which read "A single conversation across the table with a wise man is better than ten years mere study of books". You can't however go to the library and borrow a wise man to have a conversation with you.

Wednesday 19th March

Jenni decided she'd rather have her nose pierced because 30 seconds of pleasure is too fleeting to taste and then have snatched cruelly away.

I asked Ian if he's got a name for his penis. Then I let him read the bit in Forever when Ralph the penis makes an appearance. He's thinking of a name for it.

After school we went to Jacksons. I got some lime green embroidery thread to make a friendship bracelet for Shot. She said her fave colours are fluorescent ones, in a cool X-Ray Spex/Sex Pistols album cover kind of way, not a lame Wham! Wake Me Up before You Go-Go video kind of way obviously.

Thursday 20th March

Ian's penis is called Armadillo. He's named it so he can say there's an armadillo in his pants and it's really quite frightening, like Nigel Tufnel does.

I'm listening to Ice-T. Donna Harlow lent me her Ice T Power album and I lent her my Bodycount album. I wonder what Ice-T calls his penis? I bet he calls it "Evil Dick" like the song or he's got a really cool rap guy kind of name for it. There's a song he does called L.G.B.N.A.F which stands for Let's Get Butt Naked And Fuck!

Friday 21st March

I spoke to Barry today! I was wearing my Anthrax I Am The Law T-shirt and walking slowly past where he was working and he looked up and said "Great T-shirt".

Then I said "Thanks, I love the 'thrax" (I have no idea why I suddenly abbreviated Anthrax, I was just very flustered).

Then he said "Ever seen them live?"
Then I said "No" and was just about to add that my Mum probably wouldn't let me but one of the other builders called him over so I said "See you later".
Today is the last day of school until after Easter. Over the holidays I am going to have to come up with a better seduction tactic than walking slowly past.
My period started, my seventh ever, maybe the lucky seventh one will make my boobs grow. Why didn't they tell us about periods in Brownies? The handbook is supposed to be full of everything young women need to know. Also can dogs tell when you've got your period? On my way home today a dog almost strangled himself with his lead trying to get at me. At least I'm popular with dogs!

Saturday 22nd March
Re-reading yesterday's entry I realise that "the 'thrax" isn't even an abbreviation for Anthrax, it's one letter longer. I think I just had to say something because it felt like my heartbeat was so loud Barry would be able to hear it.
Mum is obsessed with the national lottery. I'm going to make money from my talents, not from chance. I don't know which talents yet but that's just a detail. It's only people who don't understand Maths who can get properly excited by the lottery (I don't understand most of Maths but I do understand probabilities and odds because of Grandad Howard explaining betting on the gee-gees to me when I was small). It's more likely that you'll get to sleep with the singer of your favourite band than that you'll win big on the lottery, but Mum hasn't got a favourite band.

Sunday 23rd March
Mega lie-in then round to Jenni's.
My Gods List:
Pete Steele
Glenn Danzig
Max Cavalera
Ice-T
Rob Zombie
Sean Yseult*
Zodiac Mindwarp
Dave Lister
David St Hubbins
Jurgen Thor

I would be a better girlfriend for Lister than Kochanski. I'd be happy to spend all my time in his bunk eating curry and having fantastic sex.
Max Cavalera has awesome hair at the moment. It's pink and dreadlocked. I bet Mum will say I can't have my hair like this until I leave school.

*is it weird to have Sean Yseult and Rob Zombie on the same Gods list? They used to be a couple but now aren't, but they are still band mates so they must be okay with each other.

Jenni's Gods List:
Twiggy Ramirez
Marilyn Manson
Pete Steele
Robert Smith

Johnny Depp
Trent Reznor
Nick Cave
Shirley Manson
Kiefer Sutherland
Dani Filth

Monday 24th March
Today is the first day of the Easter school holidays. Hooray! I'm bored of that place. Why don't my boobs look like Elvira's yet? All around me stuff like daffodils and tulips are managing to reach their potential, why can't I? Maybe after Easter they will.
Jenni is staying home all day doing her homework and Ian is playing Doom with Matty Bateman. I finished reading Philip Pullman's Northern Lights. It was okay but I think there was a lot of religious sub text I wasn't getting because I don't know that sort of stuff. Dad is an atheist and Mum is very casually religious. It had a big bear in it and it reminded me of C.S. Lewis a bit.

Tuesday 25th March
Spent all day round Ian's. Ian's brother Gav has said that Ian can listen to his records if he is very careful with them, if he puts them back *exactly* where they were, and if he doesn't take them out of the house. This is amazing. We now have a whole bunch of new stuff to listen to. It's not all metal but Gav has tons of music so some of it must be good. There's some rock stuff and some punk. Today we listened to Ted Nugent. He has the eyes of a mad man. His song "Thunderthighs" is like a horrible version of AC/DC's "Whole Lotta Rosie".

I wonder what bra size Rosie is? Do men prefer it if you're slimmer with smaller boobs, or fatter with bigger boobs?

Wednesday 26th March
Kerrang! had James Hetfield on the cover today. When will they learn that Megadeth are better and that short hair Metallica is generally bad Metallica?
Annoying neighbourhood watch fanatic Mr Moffat from number 108 stopped Mum on her way home from work to tell her he'd seen me smoking. I told her his old eyes must have been mistaken. He is an Olympic standard curtain twitcher. I'm not sure if she believes me or him.

Thursday 27th March
I saw an ice cream van today, spring is on the way. I'm still waiting for my chest to burst forth. Jenni and I went to the big Asda with her Mum and helped to do the shopping then we had a chocolate cake with mini eggs on and a drink in the café. Jenni's parents don't do the lottery, which is good because the queue for it was massive. In some ways winning the lottery would be good, I wouldn't have to worry about failing my GCSEs but it wouldn't make me less shy or larger chested (unless I bought a boob job but I don't want to do that, Mrs Butler's magazines are full of terrible tales of popped implants and massive scars).

Friday 28th March
Good Friday
Ian and I went to see his Nan Betty. She made us hot cross buns with real butter. We never have real butter at home because Mum is almost always on a diet.

Dilemma for Ian: Would he rather never play Doom again or never wear trousers again?
He's having a think about it.
This evening I watched my video of The Tale of the Bunny Picnic. The moral of the story is that sometimes it's good to be small, and you still have a part to play. I painted my nails alternating black and red, ready for the pub tomorrow.

Saturday 29th March
Ian said never wear trousers. What he'd do is wear really, really, really, really long shorts.
The Green Man was both brilliant and terrible tonight. There was too much Alanis Morissette on the Green Man jukebox. It's not even metal, give it a rest.
I saw Barry the builder! He said hello! He was with a group of mates, two men and two ladies. He's probably got a girlfriend but maybe not because of the eyebrow. It's his fatal flaw, like Macbeth's ambition. He asked me who I was with and I said just some mates (I nearly said some mates from school and then I remembered I was in the pub).

Sunday 30th March
Easter Sunday
A new TV Channel started today. It's called Channel 5 (not very imaginative) and the Spice Girls are on it so I'm not watching it. Me and Dad went to see Nanny Howard. We took her some daffodils. She was really chuffed and made a big fuss of putting them in her crystal vase. It's nice to have one Nan who has not gone a bit doolally.

She gave me a fiver to get an Easter egg or something else if I wanted. She said she wasn't sure if I was too old for an Easter egg. She reminded me of the time when I was five and Dad put some jelly egg sweets on my bedroom shelf before I went to bed and told me they were magic eggs and I shouldn't touch them. While I was fast asleep he swapped them for those fluffy yellow chicks that you decorate Easter cakes with. I was convinced they had hatched from the sweetie eggs. When Dad and I left (just before Songs Of Praise, which she watches religiously every week) I noticed she already had a load of daffodils in her garden. I think Nan's story about the eggs indicates that I could be trusted in the garden of Eden, at least for a bit.

Monday 31st March
Easter Monday
I had a Crème egg and a Spira for breakfast. I used the Spira fingers to scoop out the eggy centre. It was well lush. At the moment there is an advert that asks how do you eat yours? I think my way is the best way.

April

Tuesday 1st April
I spent all day at Ian's house. It is always relaxed and quiet compared to my house. At home sometimes Mum is fine and at other times she gets angry about nothing and starts shouting about how I don't appreciate all the things she does for me and how I'm just like my Dad. Terry had the day off work today. He is always nice to me and never makes me feel like I'm a nuisance. He has loads of nicknames for me: Ginger Tom, Goldilocks and Taylor (after Liz Taylor who was Cleopatra in an old film). Today Ian and I did a bit of our CDT coursework. We have to hand it in after Easter. It's a technical drawing of the house we want to live in, on A3 paper. Terry tried to help. Ian's house has a computer room and a room for playing guitar in. My house has a massive wardrobe and a cocktail bar. We have to do the garden too. Mine is having Cleopatra rose bushes. Terry made us cheese omelette and baked beans for lunch. In the afternoon we listened to some of Gav's records. He has loads of stuff I've seen on the Green Man jukebox but not heard. Today we tried out Marillion's Misplaced Childhood. It was too slow, apart from "Lavender" which is quite a good pop song. The trouble with liking thrash metal is you get impatient with other music because it takes so long to warm up.

Wednesday 2nd April
I went to the library today. I got Enid Blyton's In The Fifth At Mallory Towers and The Strange Case of Dr Jekyll and Mr Hyde by Robert Louis Stevenson (I like the Ozzy song "My Jekyll Doesn't Hide"). I also got two books about gardens and one about houses to help with my CDT coursework.

I had Christmas pudding that Mum bought home from work, going cheap. It's nicer when you have it at this time of year, at Christmas it's just another similar to mince pies and Christmas cake thing.
I'm listening to Pop Will Eat Itself's Box Frenzy album. I don't even care that it's not metal, it's brilliant.

Thursday 3rd April
I went to Jenni's today. Her Dad is letting her use the computer for her coursework. I asked Mum if we can get a computer. She asked what for? I said school work. She said there is a computer in the library for school work and pen and paper has worked fine for years, why change it now? She doesn't like computers because she thinks they put people out of work. There are some new computer tills in the shop where she works stacking shelves and packing bags.
Ian doesn't have a computer so he goes round Matty's to play on his. He and Gav really want one. Jenni's Dad only has one because of his job. I expect everyone will get bored of them soon anyway so there's not much point learning how to use one.

Friday 4th April
Ian is knackered today because he was up late playing Doom. I am knackered today because I was up late reading The Strange Case of Dr Jekyll and Mr Hyde. I think it shows that you shouldn't muck about in Chemistry.
Mum bought Fiendish Faces yogurts home from work. I had a raspberry one with a Bourbon biscuit dipped in it, it was lush. If I was in charge of yogurt pot design at the Fiendish Faces factory

I'd do a Dr Jekyll and Mr Hyde two faced special edition yogurt pot.

Saturday 5th April
The Green Man was brilliant. Lex and Mopey Dick were out so Jenni was well chuffed. Mopey said to me "So I assume you're virgo intacta?" and I said "No I'm Pisces, but I think all that horoscopes stuff is bollocks" and everyone laughed. Then later Jenni explained that he was asking if I've done it yet. For once I'm glad I didn't understand, because I'd have gone red. I sat next to T-Reg and he told me he had quite a good view down my top! I was pleased he was looking. He smells so lovely it makes me lightheaded.

Sunday 6th April
I had to quickly finish an essay about Macbeth and his fatal flaws, ready to hand in tomorrow. If I've got a fatal flaw it's shyness and small tits. Did Shakespeare ever cover this in his plays? No? Well then he's not still relevant today is he? Miss Wallace says he is but I can't see it myself.

Monday 7th April
Back to school, still a 32A. On my way home today I walked past the sports centre. Barry saw me and asked if I'd learnt anything good today? I said it was the same as usual, nothing as useful as bricklaying. I have learnt that I missed his lush face, Dear Diary. I'm reading In The Fifth At Mallory Towers by Enid Blyton. I can't believe that these girls are about my age.
"'Oh it's good to be back again isn't it?' said Darrell to Sally. 'I never laugh anywhere like I do at school, never!'"

They want to try going to the pub or watching Red Dwarf. They mainly get excited about swimming, horses and midnight feasts. Their school nurse is called Matron, which makes me think of Carry On films.

Tuesday 8th April
Donna Harlow is wearing a scarf because she has a massive love bite.
Something really embarrassing happened today. Ugh! I don't know if I can even tell you, Dear Diary. I was walking to the shop in the rain and I walked past this man. As I was walking past a raindrop got in my eye and so I shut my eye, but it looked like I was winking at him! He smiled at me, a really big smile, and I walked to the shop as fast as I could then I stayed in there for ages pretending to look at things. How come my body is so stupid it can't talk to people I like but will wink at total strangers who don't even have long hair?

Wednesday 9th April
All the girls were doing a "Which Spice Girl Are You?" quiz today in Maths. I was tempted to join in just to avoid doing any work. I'd got stuck again. In Maths I'm not only mentally stuck, I'm also physically stuck between Mark Dobbs and Janine Sackett because Mr Kennedy decided to randomise the seating arrangement and not do the usual alphabetical order. Mark had a copy of Fiesta in his bag. I caught a glimpse of something hairy. I don't want to be in Fiesta (Mum would go batshit crazy) but I'd like to look like I could be in Fiesta if I wanted.
The percentage of actual Maths done today was low. Mr Kennedy always begins the lesson by giving us a worksheet which he

fleetingly explains. Then he sits at his desk and leaves us to get on with it. Sometimes he leaves the room for a while and everyone gets up and wanders around, chatting to their mates.

I went to Ian's after school. We listened to Gav's Tom Petty and the Heartbreakers Into The Great Wide Open album. I think "Learning To Fly" is a great song.

I read some more of In The fifth At Mallory Towers. They are proud of things like their golden hair and their needlework but not once has one of them commented on what great tits she or another girl has. Also, none of them ever get their period.

Thursday 10th April

Maths was terrible today. We did an exercise where we had a hypothetical donkey tied to a pole in the middle of a field and we had to work out how much grass he can get to with a certain length of rope. Why make Maths harder with hypothetical donkeys? I hope Mr Kennedy gets reported to the hypothetical RSPCA.

Why do I need stupid GCSEs anyway? I bet Blackie Lawless hasn't got GCSEs. Also, I bet when Chris Holmes joined WASP no one asked him about his GCSEs, they just asked could he drink vodka and could he play guitar, in which case I'm already fifty percent qualified.

Also, I caved in and did the Spice Girls quiz. Apparently I'm Baby Spice, the blandest spice of all.

Friday 11th April

I finished a project in Textiles today. I made an owl out of two pom-poms, some pipe cleaners, a diamond shaped red bit of felt and two gold buttons from Nanny Howard's button tin. Textiles works better if you can afford to bring stuff in from home, otherwise all you've got to work with is what the school can afford to provide.

Ian asked me how important length was to women today. I said I wouldn't snog anyone with short hair.

Saturday 12th April

Ian didn't want to go out tonight until Xena Warrior Princess was over. She looks like Manowar's sexy lady cousin. I asked if he'd set his armadillo on her. He said she would definitely get a mauling as long as she put her sword down first. She could probably chuck him over her shoulder and carry him off, he's tall but skinny.

Lots of Meatloaf was played in the Green Man tonight (not by us, we have good taste). Mopey Dick said his palate was too refined to drink the cheap red wine most pubs serve. Lex said he is happy with snakebite and black. Ella asked Lex if Goths use black condoms. He said he always discusses contraception with the woman he is sleeping with and he's never used a black condom. Lex kissed Jenni's hand tonight when he was leaving.

On the way home Ian said when he asked about length yesterday he wasn't talking about hair. I said he should ask Ella or someone who knows. I told him that sometimes in Mrs Butler's magazines there is a problem about a man worrying he's too small and also sometimes from a woman who says her boyfriend is too big, but the advice is always be reassuring if he thinks it's small and relax and do it slowly if it's big. He told me I am full of wisdom and hugged me for ages at the big hedge.

Sunday 13th April

I should probably have a favourite wine by now, in case I get asked out to dinner.

Me and Dad went to see Nanny Howard. It was sunny so we sat outside in her back garden. I had a can of Dr Pepper with a straw made of paper. Some of the stuff in Nan's cupboard looks like it's been there for decades. She asked me what I'd been doing and I said school and homework. I asked what she'd been doing. She said Derek Wilton had died. He's from Coronation Street, Dear Diary, not a real person. She said it was very sudden and it makes you think. It didn't make me think, but I don't watch Coronation Street.

When I left Nanny gave me a pile of magazines to give to Mum and told me to give Mum her best wishes. Usually we don't mention Mum. When I gave Mum the magazines and the best wishes Mum said "Well, she's changed her tune". I made Mum a cup of tea then I went upstairs.

Monday 14th April

Poem for Barry:
An Adonis with hair like Curly Wurlys,
I would do anything to be your girly.
I go out of my way to walk past your lair
And when you are not there, I despair.
Your tall figure of black T-shirted mystery
Makes me late for getting to Chemistry
Your denim jacket wraps you like I wish my arms could
If only my chatting up technique was any good
I'd fill your thermos with love, not tea,
If you would go out with me

Will you build for me a mighty erection?
I'd try not to be shy when having an inspection.
You're delicious, please grant me my wishes
Maybe when I'm bustier, you will be lustier.

It needs work but it's a great start. I'm not happy with the "walk past your lair" bit but it's better than writing "the sports centre". Also it's quite a frisky ending and the rhyme scheme changes which makes it more interesting for the reader (not that I'm going to show it to anyone but you, Dear Diary). Barry rhymes with marry but that's a too obvious rhyme and anyway, steady on.

Tuesday 15th April
I've decided my favourite wine is sparkling. Ideally cherry flavour but peach will do. Matty Bateman farted with a noise like a creaking door today. He said his arse is haunted. Sally Walker admired my Danzig T-shirt today. She sometimes wears a Guns N' Roses T-shirt but I don't know if she actually likes metal.
Ian and I listened to Journey's Greatest Hits. We found it a bit wussy. Ian said he'd put it on if he had Ella or Lizzie in his room but I can have Slayer because I appreciate good music.

Wednesday 16th April
Mark Dobbs was wearing a T-shirt featuring a pair of fornicating pigs and the words "Makin' Bacon" today. Mrs Savage told him to wear something different tomorrow. We don't have a uniform but we are meant to wear appropriate clothing*. The thing is, Dear Diary, this is a very appropriate T-shirt for Mark Dobbs. Last year when we were all mucking about in Physics because our supply teacher hadn't turned up he was judged the student most

likely to end up doing porn films. We went round the room deciding who was most likely to do what. Ian was most likely to end up in a band. Jenni was most likely to be a brain surgeon. Donna Harlow was most likely to get pregnant. Sally Walker was most likely to work in Boots (she always wears so much make up it looks like her face is shouting). I was most likely to write a book and fail Maths. People ask me for help with English, but never with Maths.

It was English last lesson today. Miss Wallace said Mark Dobbs' T-shirt showed one of the more difficult uses of an apostrophe.

I bought Kerrang! on the way home. It has Machine Head, Korn and a tiny bit of Type O Negative and Napalm Death.

*The clothing I wear is appropriate to someone who loves metal. I never wear anything with a swear word on because that's asking for trouble. I like to remain under the radar of teachers where possible.

Thursday 17th April

I went to the shop and got a Bounty for breakfast. I shared it with Ian. I wonder if we're ever eating a Bounty at the same time that Alice Cooper is eating a Bounty? It's unlikely because when we're eating a Bounty at eight thirty in the morning in England, it's two in the morning in Arizona, where he lives.

Friday 18th April

If I was Alice Cooper I'd probably be up at two in the morning, eating a Bounty. He doesn't have French first thing on a Friday to worry about.

Today was a brilliant day at school. Barry the builder told me to have a good weekend.
Any idea why old people always say "Thank Crunchie it's Friday", Dear Diary? Also, is TFI Friday busier on Fridays? If so do the staff say ONI Friday (Oh No It's Friday)?
In the evening my period started. Mum bought me a Maverick bar. It's new but it's just like a Fuse really. We watched "Have I Got News For You". The eco-warrior Swampy was on it. Mum said it's possible to save the environment and have clean hair. Her priorities are seriously skewed. Even if we were the last two people alive on the planet after nuclear meltdown, like in Z For Zachariah, she would still make me brush my hair before leaving the cave to hunt for berries.

Saturday 19th April
I got ready to go to the pub (jean shorts, red leopard print tights, Slayer T-shirt) and Mum said I wasn't allowed to wear leopard print or jean shorts or any shorts until I'm eighteen. She says they make me look like a streetwalker. I asked what a streetwalker was and how come she knows so much about them.
She told me not to be so cheeky or I wouldn't be going out anywhere until I'm eighteen. I changed into black jeans then went out and met Jenni and Ian. There are women in the Green Man wearing much more exciting stuff than I want to wear, I've seen women in corsets, PVC dresses, really low cut tops and really short skirts.
Ella told us she'd seen a penis this week that reminded her of a Mars Bar. It sort of had the same veins as a Mars Bar has chocolate ripples. Lizzie said she won't want to eat Mars Bars

now. T-Reg asked me if I'd like a nibble of his Mars Bar! Everyone giggled.
If I'm not allowed to wear any shorts how will I do P.E.? This thought has cheered me up. Let's see what Mum says when I ask her to write my excuse note. I bet I'd be allowed to wear tracksuit bottoms like the Muslim girls so I'd still have to do it. Arse.

Sunday 20th April
I walked to the shop to get the Sunday People for Mum and a couple of boys started playing air guitar at me and saying "My sister's a greaser". That Clearasil advert hasn't been on for years you outdated and unoriginal pratts. I watched my Newman and Baddiel at Wembley video to cheer myself up.

Monday 21st April
Platform trainers have been banned from school due to a spate of twisted ankles. I blame the Spice Girls. One of the few good things about my school is that we don't have a uniform so we can wear normal clothes but people need to not push it too far. Today is the Queen's birthday. I hope she got to do some cool stuff instead of just walking about shaking hands with people and showing an interest. If I was the Queen I'd get all my favourite bands to play for me on my birthday and then have a massive trifle and not eat the fruit at the bottom because I'm the Queen and can do as I like. I'd also get a gold leopard print dress made specially and a giant Viennetta.

Tuesday 22nd April
We made rocky road today in Home Ec. It was really easy, even the kids who shouldn't be allowed near cookers managed it. I'm

going to make it again because it's lush. This, Dear Diary, is how you do it:

Rocky Road Recipe

100g unsalted butter or margarine
225g plain chocolate, broken into pieces
2tbsp golden syrup
2tbsp cocoa powder
2tbsp caster sugar
50g glace cherries
100g mixed milk and white chocolate chips
100g mini marshmallows
225g ginger biscuits or digestive biscuits, broken into pieces
optional 50g walnuts
Icing sugar to dust

Method
1. Line a 20cm square cake tin with greaseproof paper.
2. In a small pan, heat the butter/marg, plain chocolate, golden syrup, caster sugar, cocoa powder and stir together with a wooden spoon. When melted together leave to cool for 10 minutes.
3. In a large bowl, place the glace cherries, milk and white chocolate chips, mini marshmallows, biscuits and nuts if used and bind together with the melted chocolate sauce.
4. Pour into the lined tin and leave to set in the fridge for a minimum of 2 hrs.
5. Remove from tin and cut into pieces.
6. Dust the rocky road with icing sugar to serve.

I wonder if Barry likes rocky road?

Wednesday 23rd April

Mark Dobbs is wearing a T-shirt which says "Stop your grinnin' and drop your linen" today. Mr Murray saw it and asked him to keep his jumper on.

Kerrang! Have put the Foo Fighters on the cover but I had to buy it because it also has Type O Negative. Black Sabbath has reformed! This is brilliant news. I expect we'll soon be hearing no more of the Foo Fighters, now that the originators of heavy metal are back in business. That sounded quite good, didn't it Dear Diary? Do you think I could be a metal journalist one day? Imagine the people you'd meet.

Thursday 24th April

Just realised that to be a metal journalist I'd have to speak to people. Today Barry said hello to me and I said hello back and then I ran out of stuff to say.

Gods list:

Glenn Danzig

Pete Steele

Ice-T

Max Cavalera

Tank Girl

Rob Newman

Zodiac Mindwarp

Dave Mustaine

David St Hubbins

Dave Lister

Friday 25th April

We had a supply teacher in Biology and they made us set fire to a peanut. We pointed out we'd already done this but they made us do it again. We did it quickly so we time to muck about at the end of the lesson. I went to Ian's after school. We had toast and pineapple jam. We listened to all of Gav's Black Sabbath records, including one I hadn't heard before called Heaven and Hell. It has Ronnie James Dio, from Dio singing. It's got angels smoking on the front.

Mrs Butler called in with some magazines for Mum. Apparently fake tan is the next big thing. There's nothing much in the problem pages. Lots of the advice seems to be to talk about it. If your problem is that you go all silent around people you like then the problem and the solution are all mixed up in one.

Saturday 26th April

We put the Black Sabbath song "Heaven And Hell" on the jukebox in the Green Man. I was glad to get out of the house because Mum is in a foul mood. She always gets grumpy before and after I see Dad and then she calms down again. Depending on what mood Mum is in, Dear Diary, I've been punished by being grounded for a week for relatively minor stuff like being caught smelling of cigarettes and then bought pizza for the big stuff like being hours late home. Now I decide what's wrong and what's right without checking with Mum because surely right and wrong don't depend on the mood you're in? I got grounded a lot last year, Dear Diary. I think Mum was lonely when Dad left. I spent a lot of time on my own in my room and I think that's why I'm so shy now. While everyone else was out learning how to talk to boys and people they don't know, I was sat in my room, reading.

Last summer I missed out on a lot of drinking vodka in the park on a Friday night. After a while I realised Mum couldn't actually do anything to stop me from going out so I stopped paying any attention to the groundings and just told Mum where I was going (approximately) and when I'd be in. I'm scared it's left me a bit weird. I can spend ages on my own without really minding and I sometimes feel lost when I'm surrounded by people in the pub.

Sunday 27th April
Me and Dad went to see Nanny Howard. We watched the Grand Prix. You don't pronounce it how it's written, Dear Diary, the x is silent. This is why French is so much harder than German. German doesn't bugger about. They have words like handschuhe (glove) and schlafsack (sleeping bag), very sensible words, whereas French is sprinkled with extra letters that you don't say. It was Grandad who liked the Grand Prix, but Nan still watches it, she says she likes the noise, it's very restful.

Monday 28th April
Today has been a totally rubbish day. I found out that the building work on the sports centre is almost finished. This means no more Barry.
Barry facts:
He is nineteen
He smokes Embassy No. 1
He thinks being a builder is okay
He drinks tea (he has a thermos flask that his Mum fills for him to bring to work)
He likes Exodus, Motörhead, Metallica, White Zombie (I'm basing this on his T-shirts)

He has seen Slayer live
He is hairier than the average man (I'm basing this on his overgrown eyebrow, it honestly looks like Bert from Sesame Street's eyebrow. It's a good job I'm not the kind of shallow woman that this sort of thing bothers, Dear Diary, and I can see past his massive eyebrow, but if it gets much longer I fear he won't be able to).

Would it be easier to get close to him if I was David Attenborough and the BBC was paying me to observe builders in their natural habitat?

Tuesday 29th April
I've realised I could never be David Attenborough because I'm almost allergic to those beigey trousers he wears. Mum made me try some on once and I swear I felt hot and uncomfortable and like I was getting a rash.
After school Ian and I watched Hammer Horror's Countess Dracula. Both of us would currently be at risk of being slaughtered by henchmen to fill Countess Bathory's bathtub. Ian asked if we were in her castle and the only way to escape getting our throats slit was to shag each other, would I? I said yes obviously having sex with him is preferable to death, but it would be weird. He said we could run into a fancy bedroom with a four poster bed that had curtains and lock the door.
After Ian left Mrs Butler called round with some magazines for Mum. Problem pages included: my daughter is marrying an unsuitable man, my husband might be having an affair, I have a moustache and my boss is always mean to me. I spent a couple of

minutes checking I don't have a moustache. I don't. But, if I get one, I know what to do.
I think I'd like to do it in a four poster bed, Dear Diary.

Wednesday 30th April

I was just saying hello to Barry this morning and he got called away by a grumpy builder who said "Stop talking to the jailbait and get some work done, we've got to be finished in less than a week". In some ways I'm very insulted to be called jailbait, because it was just assumed that I'm under sixteen, without grumpy builder checking, and actually I'll be sixteen in only ten months and I think I look sixteen now and so do all the newsagents in the vicinity because they all serve me with cigarettes. But, at least he thought I was shagworthy enough to be jailbait, so it's not all bad. If Barry and I are meant to be together all the grumpy builders in the world won't be able to keep us apart.

Me and Ian listened to Gav's Quiet Riot's Metal Health album. This is one of the best things in Gav's collection so far. Terry came upstairs and gave us a Mars Bar each. We looked at the chocolate ripples and giggled. I like to bite the caramel off first and then eat the nougat bit. Ian and I both think that sometimes Ella likes to say things which she thinks will shock people.

Mum bought home some new low fat Walkers Lites crisps today. She is always on a diet, I blame the magazines she reads, no-one in Kerrang! goes on a diet because diets are very boring. If she eats chocolate she says she's being naughty, I can think of a whole load of ways I would like to be naughty and chocolate is not one of them.

Did you know, Dear Diary, that the Mars Bar was first made in Slough, which is near Reading, and that the police made up lies about what the Rolling Stones and Marianne Faithfull were doing with Mars Bars in the nineteen sixties?

May

Thursday 1st May

Miss Douglas saw me chatting to Barry today and made me help her carry some balls. If it wasn't for Barry I would be nowhere near the sports centre and would be safe from ball based errands. Miss Douglas said I should find a sport I like, so that when I leave school I can stay healthy. I thought of asking her if shagging was a sport but obviously I didn't. I escaped as soon as I could.

How annoying are Blur? I'll tell you Dear Diary, they are very annoying and "Song 2" is especially objectionable. I only mention them at all because they assaulted my ears while I was in HMV buying WASP's new album. It's called Kill Fuck Die. The first track really, really reminds me of Nine Inch Nails "Head Like A Hole" which I guess is what they were going for now they've gone industrial. There was a cute guy working in HMV wearing eyeliner and nail varnish but my heart belongs to another, Dear Diary. I'm going to tell Jenni about him though.

I read some of the Brownie Guide Handbook. Some of it is quite good and we could do with people having a more responsible attitude, lending a hand where needed, tidying up after ourselves and being capable. Some of it goes a bit too far. "A brownie always thinks of others before herself". Always? This could lead to some very angry women who never get what they want.

Friday 2nd May

There is a new prime minister. Tony Blair has replaced boring old John Major. I'd rather Lemmy from Motörhead was in charge. When I'm old enough to vote hopefully there will be some more

appealing prime minister choices. Today was Barry's last day. He said "See you around Red". School is now plunged back into mainly monotony with the occasional bright glimpse of T-Reg.
Jenni gave me this dilemma: Grow C cup boobs and a moustache or remain a non-moustachioed A cup?
My clarifying questions: Is it a big moustache or just a light one?
Jenni's answer: It's identical to T-Reg's.
My question: Are moustaches for women the next big thing (because I really don't think it's going to be fake tan, like Mum's magazine thinks)?
Jenni's answer: No, they are not.
I decided I'd rather be small of breast and hairless of top lip.

Saturday 3rd May
We've won the Eurovision Song Contest. I say "we", Dear Diary, but I mean England. I had nothing to do with it. If I'd been involved we'd have had a metal song. The Green Man tonight had T-Reg, STF, Bob, Lizzie and of course regular customers me, Ian and Jenni. I like having a boozer where I can be a regular, it makes me feel like one of the flat cap extras in Coronation Street, or like I'm in a perkier version of Cheers. Friends can keep their coffee shop (everyone except me, Jenni and Ian seems to love this programme).
Lizzie put three songs from Kiss's Crazy Nights album on. She is obsessed with Gene Simmons. She was wearing her Kiss army T-shirt too. There is no need to ask who is at the top of her Gods list. She said Ella is on a date tonight with a man with tattoos. Everyone wants a tattoo when they are old enough. Jenni wants a flock of bats, Ian wants a flaming V guitar, Lizzie wants a rose like Paul Stanley's, STF wants a big black tribal tattoo like Kerry King,

T-Reg wants a pin-up girl with her tits out, Bob wants a demon and I don't know what I want. One of my favourite things is Viennetta but I don't think this would make a good tattoo, but then again it might. I think a Viennetta, viewed sideways, is rather beautiful.

Sunday 4th May
I cleaned Mustaine out this morning. I put him in the bath while I washed out his bowl. He just used a tiny bit of the available space to swim in. If Mum wanted to she could work somewhere else instead of moaning about her job all the time. She could wear clothes that aren't beige. She could do fun stuff at weekends instead of housework and watching telly.

Monday 5th May
Today is a bank holiday. Jenni and her Mum have gone shopping in Henley. Ian came round. Mum was at work doing overtime. I made us beans on toast, with Marmite on the toast and some cheese on top. It was lush.
I'm still re-reading the Brownie Guide Handbook. I enjoyed and may put into practice the bit about being friendly but not the bit about collecting twigs. I must go to the library. There is nothing else much to read in the house except Mum's magazines or her soppy novels.

Tuesday 6th May
Today is Mum's birthday. I made her a card and I bought her some Ferrero Rocher. Mrs Butler brought Mum some special roses from her garden. I made Mum and Mrs Butler a cup of tea. I asked Mum if she wanted me to find a vase. Mrs Butler told me

the peach coloured roses were called Warm Wishes and the pink coloured ones were called Savoy Hotel. Mrs Butler told me (for the third time) that there is a rose called Cleopatra, it's red and sort of yellow as well. I cooked us macaroni cheese and Alphabites. I spelt "Mum" and "Cleo" with the Alphabites and then piled the other letters on the side of our plates. I washed up the plates and the saucepan. I have been a model daughter today. It's been quite tiring.

Wednesday 7th May
Shot lent me her Tank Girl Get Knotted graphic novel today (not a comic Dear Diary, according to Mopey Dick, who is fussy about these things). After school me and Ian listened to Gav's Anti-Nowhere League record. I think if the Sex Pistols had practised more they could have been as good as the Anti-Nowhere League. There is a Pete Steele poster in Kerrang! It's of him on the phone. I'm looking at it and imagining him saying "Just come on over any time, I like ginger women the best". If he did phone me, I just know Mum would be listening in and I'd be too shy to say anything. Actually, if it was Pete Steele I'd force myself but my voice would go all squeaky. The phone is in the hallway and I'm not allowed one in my room. I've asked a million times and said that I would only use it very occasionally. Maybe I should ask a million and one times?

Thursday 8th May
Mopey Dick told me and Jenni that heavy metal is for Neanderthal men today. This is fine with me, I like tall men. Had tea (sorry, it's called dinner round there) at Jenni's house. We had mushroom chow mein that Jenni's Mum Pam made herself. It

was really good. I didn't think you could make Chinese food yourself.

Friday 9th May
Dilemma from Ian: If you had to give up either potatoes or cheese for ever, which one would you give up?
I'm thinking about this.
I need to be more like Tank Girl. If she fancies someone she snogs them, even if they are a kangaroo. I'm more like Camp Koala. Jenni could be Jet Girl if I'm Tank Girl. How come the Spice Girls are so popular and yet Tank Girl's brilliance goes unnoticed? I might get the same tattoo as Tank Girl as well as my side view of a Viennetta tattoo.
We did reproduction in Biology today (I mean we studied it, not actually did it. Baggers has a very laissez faire approach to discipline but that would be a bit much even for him). When Baggers asked if there were any questions no one put their hand up (Biology is last thing on a Friday) except Mark Dobbs who asked if it's possible to wear your willy out? Baggers said "There have been no reported cases but I don't suggest you make that your weekend homework Dobbs".

Saturday 10th May
Boys at school think you are either frigid or a slag. There's no in between, but I am in between. With the right man I could be as frisky as Britt Ekland in The Wicker Man.
I can't decide if I'd give up potatoes or cheese for ever. Cheesy chips is one of the best meals in the known universe and probably the unknown universe too. If Marvin from Hitchhikers Guide to the Galaxy had cheesy chips it'd probably cure him of his misery.

Sunday 11th May

Today is Dad day. Nanny Howard has gone on a coach trip to see where they film Emmerdale with a load of other old people. Dad and I went to TFI Fridays. I had a chicken burger and Dad had steak. We amused each other with elephant jokes. We haven't done this for years.

Best elephant jokes:
Q. What's big, grey and wears glass slippers?
A. Cinderelephant!
Q. What's grey and highly dangerous?
A. An elephant with a machine gun!
Q. Why do elephants paint the soles of their feet yellow?
A. So they can hide upside down in the butter!
Q. Why do elephants paint the soles of their feet red?
A. So they can hide in cherry trees.
I didn't tell Dad this one because it's too rude:
Q. What's grey and comes/cums in buckets?
A. An elephant!

Monday 12th May

Natalie West asked to listen to some of Ian's music today in Maths. He let her listen to Megadeth's Countdown To Extinction. She gave it back after five minutes saying she didn't exactly like it but she didn't hate it either, she just wanted to hear it for herself. Natalie is one of the best looking girls in our year but somehow everyone likes her because she's not bitchy. She dresses in quite a trendy way but she doesn't slag off how other people dress, like Carina Norman does constantly. Carina will even be mean about what the kids who are in care and who come to school by taxi every day wear. Everyone else understands that they don't get a lot of choice and so doesn't judge them based on what they wear. Last year Mum kept threatening to put me into care but I had the contingency plan of living at Nanny Howards. I didn't tell Mum this, I wasn't sure how serious she was, some days she seemed mega serious and some days she was okay again and said she didn't know what she'd do without me.

On the way home I pointed out to Ian that he'd taken Natalie's metal virginity, he'd popped her thrash cherry. He was delighted. I didn't point out that it had only lasted five minutes and she'd given it a very lukewarm reception.

Tuesday 13th May
Donna called Carina a "Trifling Ho" in French today! Carina said that she'd heard that Donna's cousin Letitia went to the cinema with two boys and went skiing with them. Letitia is in the year above us, as is as Carina's older sister who is also a massive bitch according to Shot. I have no idea why going to the cinema and going skiing is offensive, also, how would you go skiing during term time with two boys? We aren't the sort of school that has ski trips, if we were I'd have heard about it (and avoided it, I don't like the cold or too much exercise).

Ian came round after school. I made us crinkle cut Micro Chips sandwich and Supermousse. He said I am the third best cook he knows (his Nan is first, then his Dad).

Wednesday 14th May
When I wrote yesterday that Donna called Carina a "Trifling Ho" in French I meant in our French lesson, not in the French language (we have not covered insults yet, I hope we do). Also,

Letitia didn't go actual skiing. Carina was suggesting that she had wanked off two boys at the same time, simultaneously, in the cinema, which has a sort of action that looks like skiing (apparently). Why can't people just say what they mean?
We had a supply teacher today in Chemistry. It was first lesson so she didn't really know what to do with us. She used the words problem-ette and solution-ette. Not knowing what to teach us was a problem-ette, so she wandered off in search of the solution-ette. This turned out to be reading a chapter of our textbooks. I partly did this and partly practised drawing the Anthrax logo. English was my best lesson today. Miss Wallace complemented me on my use of flowery language and wide vocabulary.
I had a problem-ette today. On the way to Ian's after school there was a massive thunderstorm and we got soaked. I borrowed a T-shirt and took my wet bra off and left it on Ian's bed to dry. I had a pair of terrible navy blue trousers in Ian's room (left from when Mum wouldn't let me wear jeans to school) so I put these on. Once dry we put on Gav's Led Zeppelin Physical Graffiti album and commenced our aural experiments. This Dear Diary, is where it gets problem-ettical, Ian's Dad Terry came up to ask if we wanted a cheese toastie (we did obviously) and he looked at the bra. Ian and I were sat at opposite ends of his bed as usual but Terry gave us a look like he thought we were up to something. We decided we'd have no more prog from this day forth, "Kashmir" was okay but the rest of the album sent me to sleep. We put Kreator's Extreme Aggression on as an antidote. It's an oasis of noise that can insulate you from all manner of teenage concerns. We practiced windmill head banging. I'd like to report

that my chest was jiggling loads and I had to put my bra back on but it wasn't, so I didn't.

Thursday 15th May

I couldn't meet Terry's eye when I called for Ian this morning. Ian said he had been given "the talk" and it was excruciatingly embarrassing. He said Terry told him that there would come a time when he noticed women and it was only natural that he would have certain urges and that he should respect women and that means not getting them pregnant and not doing anything in a hurry. Ian interrupted him and said that we got soaked in the rain and so I was wearing his T-shirt to dry off and that we're best mates but nothing more. Terry said "Yeah, for now, but things change". The thing I love about being mates with Ian is actually things don't change. Other stuff goes wrong like Mum and Dad splitting up but me and Ian are solid.

Did you know, Dear Diary that you can get ravioli that is huge squares and not in tomato sauce? We had it for dinner at Jenni's. It was chicken and spinach ravioli in a cheesy sauce.

Friday 16th May

I've finally decided. I would give up potatoes rather than cheese. Fridays at school are always brilliant, it's like everyone can taste their immanent freedom. We walk out of the school gates into the minty freshness of the weekend, ready to enjoy two days of Dionysian pleasure before heading dishevelled back through the gates on Monday morning (this is my flowery language Dear Diary, it's pretty good isn't it?).

Mum bought me some new sweets, Haribo Tangfastics. They are a bit sour and make you scrunch your face up but I like them.

Saturday 17th May

Dilemma for Jenni: If you had a tattoo on your bum would you show it to Lex and Dazza in the privacy of your bedroom?

She said yes! But, only if it was at the top of her bum, and only to one of them at a time.

At the Green Man tonight was: me, Ian, Jenni, Shot, T-Reg, Dazza and Lizzie. Ella is out with her tattooed beau again (this is the third week in a row). I've noticed that all the boys in Shot's year talk to her about serious stuff, like what they are going to do after school or if they have women trouble. She's really kind. Lizzie is sweet too, but sort of woolly headed. I can't really believe she's sixteen, she seems younger than me. Dazza moaned that they didn't have Dimmu Borgir or Emperor on the jukebox. I gave T-Reg a Tangfastic and he said it made him do his cum face!

Sunday 18th May

If you had a tattoo on your bum you'd have to show your bum to a tattooist. I don't think I'll ever have a tattoo on my bum. I mostly listened to Pantera today.

Monday 19th May

Dilemma for Ian: Would you have "Property of Natalie" tattooed on your bum if she would definitely have sex with you if you got the tattoo?
Ian's clarifying questions:
How big would the tattoo be?
My answer: about the size of a fifty pee coin.
Was he allowed to get it removed after?
Yes.

He's thinking about it.
I watched Ricki Lake. Today's problems weren't actually problems. There were some large women who liked dressing slutty and their friends were moaning. They just need new friends, problem solved.

Tuesday 20th May
Ian would get a "Property of Natalie" tattoo if it meant guaranteed sex. Ian is actually allowed to get a tattoo when he is eighteen if he wants, but his Dad would prefer him to wait until he's twenty-one. Terry has basically the same rules for Ian that he had for Gav, when Gav was his age, so it's almost like Ian already knows what he can do and what will get him bollocked. Terry's rules stay the same. They don't depend on what mood he's in, so there is no point nagging him.
Idiots at school are wearing hash leaf print T-shirts and bandanas. No one actually cares how much weed you smoke, just do it subtly and you'll get away with it. Unless of course you don't want to smoke weed, you just want everyone to think you're a bad ass who smokes weed. There's a lot of bellendrical behaviour about today.

Wednesday 21st May
Difficult Kerrang! buying decision today. It has Bon Jovi (Boo!) but also Marilyn Manson, who I'm mostly indifferent to, but Jenni loves.
We gave Gav's Kiss albums a go today. Crazy Nights gets a big thumbs down, but their first self-titled album is an amazing start for nineteen seventy four. It has "Cold Gin" and "Strutter" and gets a big horns up. Ian caused a tickle fight by saying that Danzig

would have a willy like a fun size Mars bar. I couldn't let him get away with that. Since last year Ian has got a lot stronger than me, Dear Diary.

Thursday 22nd May
I bought Kerrang! I hope Jenni knows what a great friend I am. Mark Dobbs was wearing a T-shirt that said "No Fat Chicks" today.

Friday 23rd May
My period started after P.E. I'm sure being forced to do sport messes up my insides. The Spice Girls are making being ginger a liability. Someone shouted "Oi! Ginger! Oi! Scary!" At Jenni and I today when we were in town. Some of us don't want to spice up our lives thank you very much, now zig-a-zig-off, and when you've got there zig-a-zig off some more.

List of gingers I approve of:
Cassandra Peterson (the real name of Elvira, although if I was her I'd live as Elvira all the time).
Tiffany of "I Think We're Alone Now" fame (that is a great song Dear Diary, which is why Snuff covered it, so don't go getting all "Oooh, all it's not metal, it can't be any good" on me).
Cleopatra
Tori Amos
Shirley Manson
Vyvyan from the Young Ones
Karl Logan from Manowar
Dave Mustaine
Belinda Carlisle

Carol Decker

List of bad gingers:
Ginger Spice
Ronald McDonald
Sonia

List of gingers I'm not sure about:
Chris Evans (sometimes TFI Friday is good, sometimes not)
Axl Rose (not nice to women?)
Johnny Rotten (mad eyes)
Cilla Black (it's nice that she gets people dates and surprises but I don't think she needs to do singing the same song every week)
Sarah Ferguson (nice dresses sometimes but that toe sucking thing was grim).

Saturday 24th May
The Green Man was rubbish. Ella was out, having been dumped by her tattooed boyfriend. She said he had only wanted one thing (I was sooooo tempted Dear Diary, to quote Red Dwarf:
"Arnold Rimmer: You're disgusting! You're only after me for one thing!
Arlene Rimmer: Why? How many have you got?"
But I knew it wasn't tactful so I didn't).
Mopey Dick was bitchy to Ella and essentially called her easy. He said men prize that which is rare and hard to obtain. Shot said Mopey is annoyed because he asked Ella out and she said no. She said women are every bit as entitled to sexual pleasure as men. I hate it when people argue. It reminds me of before Dad left and makes me feel miserable. Then T-Reg put his arm round Ella and

told her to cheer up and give him one of her beautiful smiles. They ended the evening snogging, Dear Diary.

Sunday 25th May

I went to see Nanny Howard with Dad. She bought me an Emmerdale pencil and some fudge back from her coach trip. She said she will enjoy watching Emmerdale even more now that she's seen where it's filmed.
I made some rocky road yesterday so I took some for Nanny and Dad. They both said it was lovely. The bit I like best is smashing up the biscuits.

Monday 26th May

In Textiles Matty Bateman farted with a noise like a mouse being run over by a motorbike. Donna Harlow said "This is meant to be creative arts not creative farts" and even Mrs Savage laughed. Josie from number 96 came round to see if we had a torch she could borrow. She wants to put some stuff in the loft. Mum said "I believe we have such an item, do give me a moment". When Mum meets someone new she does her Hyacinth Bucket (pronounced Bouquet, Dear Diary) voice but she can't keep it up for very long. While Mum hunted around for a torch Josie asked me the same questions adults always ask: What's your favourite subject at school? What do you want to do when you leave school? I said English and haven't decided. She said English was her favourite too and she has loads of books and I can go round and borrow some if I like.

Tuesday 27th May
Ian came round. We had a Wotsits and Marmite sandwich and watched Dracula AD 1972. It's set in swinging London. I'd love to visit swinging London, I think it's near Chelsea, wherever that is. Christopher Lee is brilliant in it. He doesn't say a lot, just stands about looking mean and bitey. It makes me want to put a white nightie on and leave my window open. I don't like garlic so we'd be fairly compatible. I might give up on T-Reg. I think him and Ella are going out with each other.

Wednesday 28th May
Mark Dobbs played a tune using his armpit in Maths today. It wasn't as good as Iron Maiden but it was better than the Spice Girls.
Me and Ian listened to Gav's Cinderella album. Their song "Shake Me" is just AC/DC's "You Shook Me All Night Long" again, but with added lipstick and hairspray. I need to stop having tickle fights with Ian, Dear Diary. Today he said gingers are renowned for being evil so obviously I went straight for his girly ticklish armpits but he just flipped me onto my back and I felt really weird when I was underneath him and he had my arms above my head. I'm telling you this Dear Diary, but you are sworn to absolute secrecy, I almost felt like kissing him.

Thursday 29th May
All sorts of stuff happened today Dear Diary. Donna Harlow got dragged into the boy's toilet by Mark Price. She claimed she saw Dave Chambers willy, but he said she didn't, she could only have seen his arse. Mr Murray walked past as Donna was escaping her

green tiled tinkle prison and told her off! She kept trying to interrupt him but he wouldn't let her. Mark Price said sorry to her.

Carina Norman called Natalie West fat in English today! Natalie is not fat. She has a really good figure. Ian would say it was perfect. The fattest thing in the room was Carina's bad attitude. Miss Wallace overheard and she sent Carina out! She said she would not accept a culture of bullying in her lessons (everyone else does, they just let Carina get on with being foul). Then she said that all of us will grow at different rates and every one of us is just fine as we are. Miss Wallace is such a lovely old hippy.

After ten minutes she went outside to see Carina. We all shut up so we could hear what she said to her. She told her that being unkind would get her nowhere in life, that often qualities we criticise others for are qualities we fear that we ourselves have and that if Carina is frustrated and unhappy then she can talk to her. This was not the bollocking we were hoping to hear. Miss Wallace is such a daft old hippy.

On my way home I saw Josie and went in to borrow a book. I chose Pam Ayres "Some More Of Me Poetry". Jean told me that one of her favourite Germaine Greer quotes is "A library is a place where you can lose your innocence without losing your virginity". Jean and Josie don't read Woman's Weekly, Woman or even Cosmopolitan. Jean said they present an image of womanhood that is too rigid and fixed. I think I know what she means. The knitwear models always look uncomfortable and are standing up straight, even if they are wearing a jumper described as ideal for casual cosy winter evenings.

Friday 30th May

I wonder what it would be like to lose your virginity in a library, Dear Diary? The floor would be uncomfortable but if you didn't know what you were doing you could refer to a handy reference work. But, you couldn't have a cigarette after.

Baggers told me off today in Biology. I was staring out of the window (hoping to catch a glimpse of T-Reg on his way to the sports field. My head tells me to give up on him, but my heart finds this hard) when Baggers came up behind me and slapped me on the bum with a copy of Biological Science Two. He told me to do some work. I'm glad he wasn't using the hardback edition. I said "Soz Baggers" and he said "Sorry Mr Bagnell" then I said "Sorry Mr Bagnell".

Saturday 31st May

The Green Man was so much fun tonight. T-Reg and Ella aren't going out, they are just mates. She told me herself. It was just, me, Ian, Jenni, Lizzie and Ella for a while. Ian said he loved being surrounded by gorgeous women. Ella kissed his cheek and called him a little charmer. She left a bit of a lipstick mark. Then T-Reg, Dazza and Bob came in. The conversation moved on to boobs. T-Reg said "More than a handful is a waste" and he looked at me when he said it. Then he said he can hardly fit his dick in his P.E. shorts so he feels sorry for women who are well endowed. He looked at Ella when he said this.

June

Sunday 1st June
Mum made us corned beef hash for dinner, with Viennetta for pudding. I ate not much dinner and loads of pudding. Jenni had never seen corned beef before she came to our house. It's not one of my favourites but I do like opening the tin with the little key. Mum keeps the little keys in case she ever gets a cheap tin of corned beef with the key missing.

Monday 2nd June
At school today Donna asked Miss Douglas if it's true that doing loads of P.E. makes you a lezzie? I wouldn't mind if I was one, but I'm fairly sure I'm not, but, until I've actually done it with a man I won't know for sure.
Dilemma for me and Jenni from Ian: Would you rather be used for your body or your brain? Ian and I said body, Jenni said brain.

Tuesday 3rd June
Everyone at school is wearing the same top from Miss Selfridge. These people are sheep. It's a blue T-shirt with a red heart and a thick white outline, so it sort of looks like tie-dye. There were three people in French wearing it! I was wearing my WASP T-shirt (as usual I'd smuggled it out in my bag and changed at Ian's).

Wednesday 4th June
Ian and I went to see Betty after school. She made cherry scones for us. We had them with cream and jam, they were so lush. She is definitely the best cook I know. I was trying to open the jam and she said "Righty tighty, lefty loosey". This is how you

remember which way to open things. She is full of actually useful stuff. I bet I'd learn more in a day round her house than I would in most days at school.

Thursday 5th June
Mark Dobbs had a porn mag at school! It was called Zipper. There was a smiling bloke completely starkers on a bike. It was probably a Raleigh Chopper! Mark claimed he found it in the park he walks through on his way to school when someone pointed out that it was a magazine for gay men. Mark Dobbs has previously claimed to be trisexual, meaning that he'll try anything sexual.

Friday 6th June
I saw a graph I actually understood today. It wasn't even in Maths, it was in Biology. We were doing respiration and looking at mock exam questions. There was a graph and the usual question, what does this graph tell us? Usually my answer is that it tells us that I'm crap at Maths. This time it was that smoking causes lung cancer deaths. It was just a diagonal line, with years of smoking on the x axis and risk of death on the y axis. Maybe I'm not crap at Maths, just at the sort of weird Maths we do at school. Sometimes if someone else in the class, not impatient Mr Kennedy, explains it to me, I can understand it. Like to remember which axis is the y axis, you have to remember y to the sky, because the y axis is the one that points upwards.
Mum bought me a Spira.

Saturday 7th June
Why am I still a 32A? Jenni is a 34B now. The only way I can get cleavage is by pushing my boobs together. I can't walk round

squashing my boobs together. It was me, Jenni, Ian, Shot, STF, Bob, Lex and Mopey Dick at the Green Man tonight. Mopey Dick moaned that there wasn't any Lydia Lunch on the jukebox. Shot, STF and Bob have GCSE exams next week. Shot was telling Bob and STF not to worry about them too much and to just try their best. She takes her lucky green haired punk troll with her to exams. Bob takes a packet of Marlboro and touches the upside down for luck cigarette he always creates when he starts a new packet before he goes in and STF's lucky charm is his Iron Maiden sweat band.

Sunday 8th June
Dad and I went to the Sunday market/car boot sale. The top half of the field is market stalls and the bottom half is a boot sale. He bought me some amazing pink camouflage trousers from the army surplus stall. There was just boring stuff like kitchen roll and fake Power Rangers on most of the market stalls. Almost every boot sale stall had a Chippendales video, an empty Huntley and Palmers tin (these are supposed to be collectable, Dear Diary), at least one Stephen King paperback (all his books are a film, you don't need to read them) and a copy of Rosemary Conley's Complete Hip And Thigh Diet book. Mum has this book. I don't see how a diet can specify the area which weight loss occurs from. I would read Elvira's Great Big Boob Diet but sadly it doesn't exist. Ian's Nan Betty says "If a thing sounds too good to be true, then it probably is".
We went to Nanny Howard's. I showed her my trousers but I don't think she was impressed.

Monday 9th June
I had a dream where I got hit by lightning and my boobs grew! It was like that was my superpower. I've stopped smoking.
Reasons why smoking isn't cool:
1. Not worth getting bollocked for when caught
2. Smells grim
3. Might stop boobs growing
4. Uses money that could otherwise be spent on CDs
5. The graph I saw in Biology has made smokers look like twerps.

Reasons why smoking is cool:
1. Get to hang around behind the Maths block
2. Perfect subterfuge to speak to hot men, asking someone for a light is the most natural thing in the world. Even I can manage to do this occasionally.

Tuesday 10th June
Mum said I can't wear my pink camouflage trousers to school. I have to save them for weekends. This is ridiculous! I don't have a school uniform which means basically I can wear whatever I want. My brain doesn't work better wearing shit clothes, if anything it probably works worse, because of the shame. She should see what some people wear to school. Ella was wearing a low cut halter top last week.
I played the adverts game with Ian. You have to guess what the advert is for and the one with the lowest score at the end of the ad break has to make the tea. I won the first round (I got Coco Pops, Flora, Mellow Bird's coffee and Felix cat food while Ian only got Mullerice and Pringles) but he won the second round because I didn't recognise the Sugar Puffs advert fast enough.

Wednesday 11th June

I didn't buy Kerrang! this week because Bon Jovi is on the cover. I read in Ian's Metal Hammer that Alice Cooper is playing here in England in July. I asked Mum if I can go. She said no. She says I'm not old enough to go to London on my own. I said I wouldn't be going on my own, Jenni and Ian would be coming with me. She said they aren't old enough to go either. She said maybe next year when I'm sixteen. Why does everything have to wait until I'm sixteen? I'm mature for my age. It's so unfair.

We listened to Gav's Best of the Undertones album. I wish I was getting some teenage kicks.

Thursday 12th June

Biology was good today. Baggers (sorry, Dear Diary, I mean Mr Bagnell) brought in some cow lungs still attached to the trachea and blew them up with a bellows. It was so much better than the dull stuff with plants we did last term. Jenni stood right at the front today and Baggers let her have a go with the bellows. Baggers asked how a smoker's lungs would be different and all the smokers in the class stuffed their fag packets further down in their pockets and shuffled their feet and looked at the floor. Since I'm no longer a smoker I didn't feel uncomfortable.

When Baggers was handing the lungs to the lab assistant to be taken away Carina Norman said "You'd better hide them well in the rubbish, Jenni will be looking for them to suck the blood out". Ian and I gave her loads of cut eye but as usual Jenni didn't need any help and said "I've heard you've sucked much worse" and everyone started laughing at Carina (except Janine).

I watched my Alice Cooper videos: Welcome To My Nightmare and The Nightmare Returns. My nightmare is that I'm not allowed to go and see Alice Cooper.

Friday 13th June
I wrote a note from Mum excusing me from swimming today. Carina Norman asked me loudly if Aunt Flo was visiting. I didn't have a clue what she was talking about. Donna Harlow told me after that she meant my menstrual flow, my period. She said some women call it that. Why do we need so many words for something no one wants to talk about?
Dilemma for Ian: Would you rather be caught wanking or listening to Bon Jovi? Ian said this was an invalid dilemma. He would never listen to Bon Jovi.
Harry Hill had Gary Bushell from the Gonads on tonight.

Saturday 14th June
Today is Dad's birthday. He took me to see Nan. She'd made him a lemon cake. It had tiny little sweetie lemon slices on it, like you get at Christmas in a pack with orange slices. She gave him book tokens. She always gives him book tokens. I gave him a card I'd made and some Brut aftershave. I always give him Brut aftershave. I think men over thirty wear Brut and men under thirty wear Lynx.
It's sad when we have to say goodbye. I worry about him being lonely, living on his own, going back to an empty place on his birthday. I wouldn't mind if he got a girlfriend, I understand that people have needs, but I don't know how to say this to him. When Mum and Dad first separated I didn't understand how people could stop wanting to be married, but now I've gone off

stuff that I used to love myself (rainbow legwarmers, ra-ra skirts, tap and ballet classes) I can sort of understand that people change.

I felt tired when Ian and I called for Jenni. She said I should eat stuff with iron in when I have a period. Spinach doesn't actually have loads of iron in, it has some but there was a mix up with a decimal point and people thought it had more iron than it really did. This sounds like exactly the sort of thing that happens to me in Maths.

The Green Man was crowded tonight. STF, Shot, Ella, Lizzie, T-Reg, Bob and Dazza were all out. They are about half way through their GCSE exams. STF said if he fails he'll get a job in the factory where his Mum works. Shot says she'll write graphic novels if she fails. Ella says she'll become a topless model. Lizzie said she'll do retakes. T-Reg said if he passes or if he fails he'll probably become an electrician. His Dad has got a mate who needs an apprentice. Bob said he wants to work with computers and he'll get a job doing anything with computers if he fails. Dazza said he'll start his own record label. I hope no one does fail. Everyone except T-Reg and Bob wants to do A Levels but the school will kick them out if they fail their GCSEs.

Shot made us do a toast, to friends and to being in the pub on a Saturday, no matter what we end up doing the rest of the week. When she raised her glass I noticed she is still wearing the friendship bracelet I made her.

Sunday 15th June
Today is Father's Day. I gave Dad his card yesterday with his birthday card. Jenni and Ian are both busy today doing stuff with their Dads but I'm only allowed mine every fortnight.

Monday 16th June

I asked Mum if I'm allowed to go to the Sunday of Reading Festival. It's not quite as good as going to see Alice Cooper would be but it does have Metallica and Marilyn Manson. Jenni is desperate to go. She says she'll even get a job to buy the ticket. Mum said no to me going, it's too expensive.

Tuesday 17th June

In German we had a visit from some kids that go to the school in Düsseldorf that our school is twinned with. It was a weird lesson. We didn't have to do any proper work, just talk. A couple of the German boys like metal so we talked to them. Their names are Dominik and Florian. Dominik has shiny black hair. It just escapes being a mullet because his fringe is quite long. Florian has blonde curly hair. At the end of the lesson Mr Webbley invited us all to the school disco being put on especially for the German visitors tomorrow night. Usually nothing will get me, Ian or Jenni to be on school grounds for a second longer than is necessary, but we said we'd go. It's from seven to nine and is in the hall where we have assembly.

Wednesday 18th June

This morning Ian and I listened to the Scorpions "Rock You Like A Hurricane". We had a special assembly today. I think our school is showing off because we have guests, in the same way that Mum does. I expect we aren't allowed to call the toilets "the bogs" while we've got visitors. The upper sixth German class sang! They and the visitors sang The Beatles' "She Loves You" in German. Everyone who doesn't do German was giggling at the word "dich". Actually, even people who do do German were giggling at the word "dich".

It was very weird going to school in the evening. It was so quiet compared to during the day. I feel even shyer speaking in German than I do in English. Luckily everyone stopped speaking German fairly swiftly when the visitors realised that to stick to it would mean an entire evening of being asked the way to the town hall (Das Rathaus, Dear Diary) or being told about our family pets (Ich habe einen Goldfisch namens Mustaine). The German visitors were taken to the Reading Rathaus today and went to the museum. They saw the replica Bayeux tapestry and learnt about the long biscuit making history of Reading. Once we've presented these gems we run out of exciting stuff so it's a good job the women of Reading are beautiful.

The disco was lame (I will not stay in the same room as a DJ who is perpetrating the Spice Girls) so we took Dominik and Florian for a tour round the school. We showed them the Maths block and where we smoke behind it and the sports centre which is the newest bit of the school. We sat on the field and talked about music. They said in Germany they like proper manly men like Bruce Dickinson, Wolff Hoffman and Rob Halford.

Thursday 19th June

I saw a real male nipple today, Dear Diary. After school Jenni and I we went to the park for a bit with Dazza, T-Reg and Ella who had just had a French oral exam. It was really hot and we all sat on the grass and T-Reg took his top off! I've now seen him fifty percent naked! I didn't have a really, really good look because I didn't want to stare. I wish I'd had my sunglasses with me. I have to stay covered up in the sun because I burn. Jenni won't risk getting tanned even though she could. A suntan is just not a good Goth look. After a while Dazza and T-Reg had to go. Ella stayed and chatted to us. She told us that she has had sex in this very park! She said once you've done it a few times it's not a big deal. She said her first boyfriend had said to her "If you loved me, you'd have sex with me". She said she didn't love him but she was curious so she did. They broke up ages ago and she gets irritable if she doesn't regularly have sex!

Friday 20th June
I got my period this morning. I felt dizzy and ill all evening. I now have all the types of pain you can get while having a period (bad headache, stomach pain, nausea, dizziness and backache!). Mum brought me a cup of tea and two Feminax. She made me tomato soup for dinner.

Saturday 21st June
Mum fussed about me going out tonight because I felt ill all of yesterday. I told her I was fine but if I wanted someone to fuss over me she'd be my first choice. Her fussing skills are second to none. I'm not going to miss the pub, it's my favourite part of the week.
Tonight in the Green Man we were talking about what Shot calls the wanking off disparity. She means that girls do it to boys quite a lot but you don't hear of boys doing it to girls as much.
When Ian walked me home he said maybe boys don't wank girls off as much not because they are being selfish, but because they don't know how to do it. I told him this is exactly why girls are

only interested in older boys, they want someone who knows what he's doing.

Sunday 22nd June
I watched my Punt and Dennis video this morning. Hugh Dennis gave me a great idea with his "Wonderpants" sketch. Eureka! Get a Wonderbra! Problem solved. Instant boobs while my actual ones are growing. This is the most genius idea I've had since I started changing at Ian's so I could wear normal people clothes to school and not the navy blue crap Mum expects me to wear.

Monday 23rd June
Mopey Dick high fived Jenni because Echo & the Bunnymen are at number one. It's nice to see the Goths cheerful about something.

Tuesday 24th June
Ian beat me in the advert game. I didn't get McVitie's Fruit Jaspers fast enough. I made us a cup of tea and a roast beef flavour Monster Munch and salad cream sandwich.

Wednesday 25th June
Matty Bateman farted with the noise of a flock of ducks in Chemistry today. He smirked and said "Nobody smoke" (which they wouldn't have done anyway). Kerrang! has Type O this week so I bought it instantly.
Me and Ian listened to Gav's Status Quo records. I think "Mystery song" is kind of awesome.

Thursday 26th June
I asked Mum if I could have money for a new bra. She said not until I grow out of the ones I've got. I am trying you know! It's alright for her and Nanny Brooks, they have got massive chests. I'm more like Nanny Howard, short and flat.

Friday 27th June
Maybe Dad would give me money for a Wonderbra if he didn't know what it's for. He said he would buy me a ticket to the Sunday of Reading Festival if Mum agrees I can go! I made her a cup of tea and then I asked her, but she said no. For Lemmy's sake, what is wrong with me going to see a band not five miles away from my house?

Saturday 28th June
Jenni got a black PVC skirt from New Look in the Broad Street Mall (formerly the Butts Centre because it's near St Mary's Butts, old people still call it that, Dear Diary, which always makes me giggle). I'm in a foul mood today. Jenni and Ian have tickets for Reading Festival Sunday and I don't. Jenni and her brother Bruce are going and Ian is going with them. Jenni's Mum said she doesn't have to get a job to buy her ticket. She'd rather she concentrated on her school work. They just bought her and Bruce a ticket each! Jenni's parents can afford Sky telly but choose not to have it!
I bought a birthday card for Nanny Howard. Her birthday is on Monday. I asked Mum if she'd like me to write it from both of us. She said okay.
Everyone has finished their GCSE exams.

Sunday 29th June
I mowed the lawn today without Mum asking. I have got to see Metallica and Marilyn Manson, Dear Diary.
Mum and I watched "Oh Dr Beeching!" tonight. It's a sort of railway based Hi-De-Hi. I wanted to like it. It had a lot of audience laughter but I still prefer Hi-De-Hi because it reminds me of family holidays. I asked Mum again if I could go to Reading Festival on the Sunday, I told her Jenni's brother Bruce is taking her and that he's responsible and that we can't possibly get into any trouble and her Dad will pick us up after and it's only local. Mum said she'd think about it.

Monday 30th June
It's Nanny Howard's birthday so I went to see her after school. It was weird being there on my own, without Dad. Nanny told me that when Dad didn't see me for a couple of months at the end of last year he was heartbroken. She said it'll be easier when I'm sixteen and able to make my own decisions. She is so right, many things will be easier when I'm sixteen but it's still eight long months away.

July

Tuesday 1st July
We used the Van der Graaf generator in Physics today. I was chosen to stand on the washing up bowl and have my hair stuck up. Mr Venables said he needed someone with long hair that didn't have loads of hairspray in it. I felt a right plum stood in front of the whole class with everyone staring at me.
Mum bought home some dented cans of blackcurrant One Cal. I asked her again about Reading Festival. She said I could go on the condition that I behave myself between now and then! I rang Dad to ask him to buy me a ticket.

Wednesday 2nd July
I'm so happy today. I get to go to my first gig in less than two months. Maybe next year I'll get to go to a gig in London.
I bought Kerrang! without hesitation because Alice Cooper is in it. Jenni won't like this issue though because Alice is claiming that Marilyn Manson stole his act. We'll see for ourselves in August! Me and Ian listened to Gav's The Specials album. I like "Too Much Too Young". I'm going to heed it's warning and not get married too young (or maybe at all, it looks rubbish based on Mum and Dad).

Thursday 3rd July
My bum hurts today, me and Ian went on the see-saw yesterday on our way home and he's bigger than I am, so I landed from higher up than he did. Also, me and Jenni got kicked out of Ann Summers. You have to be eighteen to look at the really rude stuff at the back of the shop. Today has not been a huge success. I

took my injured bottom and injured pride to bed early and listened to Suicidal Tendencies "You can't Bring Me Down".

Friday 4th July
Bum still hurts. Ian offered to rub it better, I declined with thanks. Carina dared Janine to stick a sanitary towel onto Mrs Savage's back in textiles today. Janine managed it and there was loads of giggling. Carina is so childish. Mrs Savage is easily embarrassed. As a fellow massive blusher I didn't want to see her have to answer the questions "What's that on your back miss? What's it for?" Charmaine Payne called Mrs Savage into the big cupboard where all the materials are kept and removed it stealthily. There are a few girls in my year whose Mums can hardly afford STs and who always have to go to the school nurse to get some.
I'm listening to Rage Against The Machine. It's got a parental advisory sticker on it.

Saturday 5th July
In the Green Man tonight T-Reg asked Lizzie if she swallowed! She slapped him and didn't answer. Lizzie has a very direct approach when it comes to dealing with unwanted attention. I wonder what spunk tastes like? It's bound to be grim isn't it? Jenni said she isn't going to swallow ever but she wouldn't mind jizz on her tits if necessary. Lizzie told me that sometimes when she hangs around with Ella she gets into situations she'd rather not be in with boys. Basically Ella is boy mad and sometimes arranges double dates which Lizzie goes on with her. Lizzie said that because Ella is quite friendly they expect her to be too. Sometimes she pretends to have a boyfriend called Paul.

Ian walked me home and asked if I wanted a go on the see-saw. I said no.

Sunday 6th July

Bum no longer hurts. Dad gave me my ticket! I'm going to see Metallica and Marilyn Manson! Dad and I went to see Nanny Howard. I told her I was going to the Reading Festival on the Sunday and she said she'd look out for me on the telly (it's always shown on the local news, with local people moaning about the inconvenience). There is a new family called the Battersbys in Coronation Street. We had lemon curd sandwiches and raspberry ripple ice cream with Ice Magic.

Monday 7th July

Carina Norman said today that people with wide taste in music are smarter than people with narrow taste in music. She thinks she has broad taste in music because she likes all chart music! By the same argument I have wide taste in music, I like thrash metal, heavy metal, a bit of death metal and some classic rock.

Tuesday 8th July

And I like The Prodigy and Pop Will Eat Itself, Dear Diary, so Carina Norman can eat my shorts.
Ian got in a huff this morning because I called Cryptic Writings "Craptic Writings". My fave Megadeth album is So Far, So Good, So What. Craptic Writings is neither punky nor thrashy enough for me. Ian is such a lover of Dave Mustaine that he can't see the evidence of his own ears.

Wednesday 9th July

I meant Ian can't hear the evidence of his own ears, Dear Diary. He is no longer in a huff because today I bought him a packet of Snaps and told him I thought Cryptic Writings was probably a grower (but I'm sure it isn't, but his childish sulks are annoying, why is everyone arguing over music at the moment?).

Thursday 10th July

Jenni and I have decided to change the way we do our Gods list. We're doing an international version and a Reading version. We struggled to get to ten on the Reading version. Actually we could each only manage two. We know way more than ten boys each but most of them we go to school with and when compared to their international counterparts they are not that appealing.

Gods list (International)
Glenn Danzig
Mille Petrozza
Pete Steele
Christopher Lee
Zodiac Mindwarp
Dave Lister
David St Hubbins
Joey DeMaio
Tank Girl
Rob Zombie

Sadly Dave Mustaine has fallen into around eleventh place due to Cryptic Writings.

Gods list (Reading)
Barry
Tyrannosaurus Reg

Jenni's Gods list (international)
Pete Steele
Marilyn Manson
Andrew Eldritch
Trent Reznor
Johnny Depp
Robert Smith
Twiggy Ramirez
Nick Cave
Morticia Addams (1960s TV version)
Kiefer Sutherland

Jenni's Gods list (Reading)
Lex
Darren

Mrs Butler brought some magazines round for Mum. I read the problem pages. If I had a boyfriend I don't think I'd mind if he wanted to try my knickers on. Also, how do you use sex as a weapon? And why shouldn't you do this?

Friday 11th July
Carina Norman called me Duracell today. For the love of Lemmy, I know I'm ginger, it's really, really old news. Mark Dobbs asked if I go all night. I just ignored him. Ian tried to cheer me up by calling me his little pink bunny.

Saturday 12th July
Ella pointed out to me tonight that T-Reg dresses on the left! She said that men who dress on the left tend to be good in bed! Ella has dyed her hair even blonder than usual. She said her inspiration is Pamela Anderson.

Sunday 13th July
Tony Blair is all over the papers. He invited a load of pop stars to a cocktail party at 10 Downing Street. Noel Gallagher went, and Vivienne Westwood who made clothes for the Sex Pistols, and Anita Roddick. I wonder if she took a Body Shop gift basket for Cherie? Tony is so desperate to not be seen as a boring old stuffy politician. He reminds me of Mr Freeman, who is always trying to prove how young and trendy he is.
Mum said at least you knew where you were with John Major. She never liked him because she always votes Labour. She did think he was sensible to start the lottery. She said it's the only way the likes of us will end up having the same sort of money as the likes of him. She said Blair looks like a loose cannon to her.

Monday 14th July
I was given a thorny dilemma from Ian today: Would I rather die a virgin or have sex with Jon Bon Jovi?
My clarifying questions:
Am I allowed to put a bag on his head?
Would anyone find out?
Can I get a mark out of ten from three different sources for how good JBJ is in bed before I commit myself?
Is it long hair eighties JBJ or short hair nineties JBJ?

I still haven't decided.

Tuesday 15ᵗʰ July
I've decided. I would rather go to my grave pure and untouched than sleep with JBJ.

Wednesday 16ᵗʰ July
Ian and I listened to Gav's Jethro Tull Catfish Rising album. It was weird. Ian's Dad Terry had a day off today. He made us gammon, egg and crinkle cut chips for tea. He is good at cooking but I suppose you have to learn if your wife leaves you. He's a better cook than my Dad. My stupid period started and I didn't have anything in my bag so I put toilet paper in my knickers and went home, claiming Mum had told me I had to be in at seven-thirty. I'm convinced my period has been brought on by the stress of thinking about boffing JBJ, it's like my body is trying to protect me from the horror.
Kerrang! Had a 100 best gigs feature this week. My Mum has so far only let me go to one. At the risk of sounding like Kevin the teenager from Harry Enfield And Friends, Dear Diary, it's so unfair.

Thursday 17ᵗʰ July
Matty Bateman did a really long and loud fart that sounded like someone dribbling a basketball today. He is truly revolting. He wasn't even embarrassed. Carina Norman said I fancy Wolf from Gladiators, because he's got long hair. I don't, but Ian does fancy Jet. Then she said Jenni fancies Pat Sharp. Jenni said it was bit sad that someone of Carina's age still watches "Fun House".

Mum bought some Virgin Cola home today, cheers Mum, I know I'm not getting lucky, what's next, Virgin bread? Virgin tea bags?

Friday 18th July
Today is a brilliant day! It's the last day of school and I've finally saved up enough for a Wonderbra! Jenni and I went to town and I got a black lace one! It has padding and extra padding. You can take the extra padding out if you want, but I'm going to keep it in, what's the point in buying a Wonderbra if you're not going to fully utilise it? I'm going to bring out the big guns, Dear Diary. We hung out in Prospect Park for a bit after we'd been to the shops. We saw Bob and Darren. Then Darren walked home with Jenni.

Saturday 19th July
I don't know if Jenni got any dazzling Darren action because she is now on holiday for a week with her parents and Bruce and Minty. It will help with her GCSE French apparently. She said she would sort of rather stay here but she also likes hanging out with Bruce and Minty.
I haven't been on holiday since Dad left. Ian hasn't been on holiday since his Mum left. We used to go to Butlin's. I'd probably find it boring now but when I was a little kid it was truly paradise. I could have as many goes on the Ladybirds, the Alice In Wonderland Train, the Galloping Horses and the other fair rides as I wanted. We went swimming in the indoor pool and in the outdoor pool. The indoor pool was made of glass so that people in the ballroom could see the swimmers. We fed the ducks in the duck pond which was lit up at night with red, blue, green and yellow light. It was one of the most beautiful things I'd ever seen,

like having fairy lights in summer. We had fish and chips. We went to a toy shop and the Bognor Regis book exchange. We had a knickerbocker glory in Wimpy. It was almost as good as Christmas, a shining diamond of a week that I never wanted to end.

I tried my Wonderbra on. I can't go out like this. People will stare. I'm stacked, but it's all smoke and mirrors. I wore my usual bra to the pub.

Sunday 20th July

I went to see Nanny Howard with Dad. Before I went Mum gave me a pile of magazines to give to Nanny with her best wishes. This is a ginormous step forward in Mum/Nan relations. When I gave them to Nanny she said "How kind, do thank her for me". Nanny Howard is small chested and Nanny Brooks is medium to large. I wonder which I've inherited. It's not too late for me to grow a wazzo pair of jugs (yes, Dear Diary, I've been watching Bottom). I found the Pogs and Tazos I'd collected years ago. I've totally grown out of these but I told Nanny to keep them. She put them with my Smartie top collection. I like having this stuff here. It reminds me of simpler times. I noticed she still has an owl, made of shells that we brought her back from Bognor Regis. When I left she gave me a Frys Orange Cream and some magazines to give to Mum. Some of the magazines are probably too fogey even for Mum to read (The People's Friend and The Lady).

Monday 21st July

Mum bought home a big bag of Opal Fruits which were cheap because the packet had got opened by mistake. I made Opal

Fruits cocktails by putting two in my mouth at once. Strawberry and lemon is my favourite. I made Mum try it. I wish I was somewhere exotic drinking real cocktails.

Tuesday 22nd July
Ian and I went round to see Betty today. Even though she's old she doesn't think people should wear boring clothes or worry about what the neighbours think. She thought Terry looked handsome when he had long hair as a teenager (it was fashionable for men to have long hair when Ian's Dad was growing up, Dear Diary, this seems unbelievable to me now) and she thinks Ian looks handsome with long hair. If anyone says anything to her about it she says "It doesn't matter what you look like. It's how you behave that's important". When Terry started growing his hair, his Dad moaned but Betty stuck up for him. Ian's hair is longer than Terry's was and isn't fashionable.
Betty sent us to the shop for cream doughnuts and fizzy pop and we sat in the garden and had a picnic. She found me a big straw hat to wear so I wouldn't get burnt. She said my complexion is beautiful, like a Pears Soap baby's face (I don't know what that is but I said thank you). Usually I'd feel daft in a big hat but since it was only Ian and Betty it didn't matter.

Wednesday 23rd July
We listened to some of Gav's records. Pete Steele claims to be influenced by The Beatles so we gave them a go. It turns out that they didn't just do soppy rubbish like "I Wanna Hold Your hand". They also did "Eleanor Rigby" which is dark and gloomy.

Thursday 24th July
Ian is playing Doom with Matty today. Mum told me to tidy my room and put any washing in the laundry basket. I started doing this but got distracted when I found my Game Boy and ended up playing Tetris for a couple of hours.

Friday 25th July
I nearly saw T-Reg's youknowwhat today! We* were all mucking about in the park, listening to music on Ella's portable CD player and he put my CD down his pants and invited me to get it back! It was dark down there and I didn't put my hand in but I saw something fleshy. It made me think of the courgettes Mrs Butler brings round occasionally.
*Me, Ian, Ella, Lizzie, T-Reg and STF, Dear diary.

Saturday 26th July
Jenni got back from holiday this morning. She went topless on a beach! So did Minty! And her Mum! Her Mum, Dear Diary! I told her about nearly seeing Reg's youknowwhat but since she'd been on a nudist beach it wasn't a great story any more.
I wore my Wonderbra out of the house for the first time. It's making stuff happen already, someone at the bar spilt a drink on me and some of it went on my top instead of straight onto my feet. We're calling it a gincident! I think T-Reg was staring at my chest. I hope it was in a good way and not in a Sherlock Holmes kind of mystified way: The case of the sudden stackedness.
Also, I saw Barry! I wasn't sure if he'd remember me, but he did and he said Hi. I asked him where he was working at the moment. He said he's doing a house extension in Pangbourne and there are no cheerful redheads to walk past and make his morning! He

hasn't seen me for a couple of months (it seems like an eternity) so he may think my chest is the genuine article. He was with two girls and two guys again and I still can't tell if he's got a girlfriend. He is absolutely gorgeous, even with the eyebrow. He was wearing black jeans and a Slayer T-shirt and looked cleaner than he does at work.

Sunday 27th July

Mum's lottery obsession has finally paid off! She got four numbers! She said I can have the fourteen hole cherry red DMs I've been on about for ages, on the strict condition that I only wear them at weekends, and she is getting a new stair carpet.

Monday 28th July

Mum collected her winnings today. When the ice cream van came she bought us both an ice cream oyster with a flake! I've never had one of these before. They are as good as Viennetta. I know I moaned about the lottery Dear Diary, and I have been guilty of calling it a tax on the poor and gullible, but it's like Mum is a different woman since she's won and she only got four numbers, imagine if she'd got more. Anything which makes people happy without making other people unhappy can't be bad.

Tuesday 29th July

I went into town and got my cherry red DMs this morning. Then me and Ian watched Basket Case. Suppose only one of my boobs grows and the other remains small, like an ill-formed mutant? We had Pot Noodle for dinner. I hope the chemicals help my chest along. I presented our Pot Noodles beautifully by cutting the bread we like to dip into them into four delicate triangles.

Wednesday 30th July
Me and Jenni got kicked out of Ann Summers again today. It was going well and we were making our way steadily towards the back of the shop where they keep the weird stuff. Jenni picked up a bra and said to me, in an even posher than usual voice "Yes, I think my husband would approve of this". The security guard came over and asked us our age and we said we were nineteen. He stroked his chin in that "I think that's total bollocks" sort of way and told us we'd have to leave and to bring ID if we want to shop there.

Thursday 31st July
We sat on Jenni's lawn and made daisy chains today. I took my new DMs off because they had given me a blister. We covered Ian in daisy necklaces and headbands. Pam came out with some cordial* for us and said we'd have loved the sixties**.
Mum has got a load of carpet samples. She asked me which I thought was the best quality one and which looks best with the colour of the hallway. I said I wasn't Lawrence Llewelyn-Bowen. She said she didn't want to get an unsuitable carpet that doesn't go. I'm sure that would be headline news in the Reading Chronicle: "Local Woman Gets Slightly Mismatched Carpet Shocker, Neighbours in Uproar".

*sounds fancy but is just squash.
**everyone goes on about the sixties but surely the seventies were better because that's when heavy metal got started?

August

Friday 1st August

Ian told me today that boys don't care how big your boobs are. He said they pretend to when they're all together but actually it's not that big a deal. Why did no-one tell me this before? He asked if women really care about how big your armadillo is. I said the things that worry me about doing it is not that at all, it's a) how much it'll hurt, b) fear of doing it wrong and being called boring in bed c) fear of getting pregnant d) fear of people finding out and calling me a slag e) being dumped straight after doing it.
It's weird how I can't talk to most men but I can talk to Ian just like I can talk to Jenni.

Saturday 2nd August

Ian invented a new metal hand gesture which he's calling the evil goat udders. You tuck your thumb in and dangle your four fingers. I don't think it's going to catch on but I haven't got the heart to tell him after he was so sweet yesterday.
T-Reg was wearing a vest tonight. He looks good sweaty. Shot said she'd had to put her eyeliner in the fridge. She still looks amazing. Ella said sunshine makes everyone horny. Lizzie told her to speak for herself. T-Reg agreed with Ella. I agree with Ella when I look at T-Reg in a vest. Lex was wearing a fishnet top tonight so Jenni had some eye candy too. Mopey Dick said he finds the stillness of the summer air deeply oppressive. He also said the acres of flesh on display are no more appealing to him than a butcher's shop window. Bob said one of the best things about summer is bird watching (he means women, Dear Diary, he's not a devotee of Bill Oddie).

Sunday 3rd August
Today is Dad day. Nanny Howard told us she wouldn't vote for Scampi. It turns out she meant Swampy the eco-warrior. He is considering standing for election. She said you've got to think about a bit more than trees to get her vote. Dad bought me some ice cream flavour Chewits.

Monday 4th August
I wanted to spend all day reading in my bedroom and listening to music but the new stair carpet is being fitted today so Mum made me get up and get dressed. She said I wasn't allowed to put any music on until the carpet fitters had gone. I have no idea why I couldn't have just stayed in my room while the carpet was being fitted and why music and carpet fitting don't mix. I decided not to ask.
Today is really hot. I'm wearing my Alice Cooper Constrictor T-shirt because it's one of the only white things I've got. I walked to the shop in this and a black skirt with no tights and got "milk bottle legs" shouted at me by an idiot on a bike. I got a blue Mr Freeze and walked home to put some tights on.
Mum is very pleased with the new stair carpet. Mrs Butler has been in to have a look. Mum asked why I was wearing tights indoors on one of the hottest days of the year. It's okay for her, she has brown hair and can get a sun tan.
During the adverts in Coronation Street this evening I came out of my room to find Mum stroking the fourth stair.

Tuesday 5th August
I made some cakes this morning. I decorated them with red icing which I made look like splatters of blood and I put vampire fang sweets on top of the icing. I took them round to Jenni's. Her Mum Pam said I was very creative. I think this is why I'm rubbish at Maths. I have a creative brain, not a Maths brain.

Wednesday 6th August
Today we sat at Jenni's kitchen table and made astrology not suck! You might wonder how we brought about this miraculous change, Dear Diary. We added the magic ingredient of heavy metal. I bet Mystic Meg didn't see that coming.
Heavy Metal astrology is similar to regular astrology (in that it's bollocks dreamed up for some diverting entertainment).
There are twelve signs, whichever one you are is dependent on the date of your birth (actual birth or when you began listening to metal). The signs are the Studded Wristband, the Skull, the Denim Patched Waistcoat, the Snake, the Leather Jacket, the Long Hair, the Cannons, the Horns, the Spooky Pumpkin, the Jack Daniels, the Cucumber and the Bat. Anyone wanting to change their heavy metal astrological sign can do so by giving me, Ian and Jenni a chocolate biscuit each. It's that simple.

Date Ranges for Heavy Metal Zodiac Signs:
21 March - 19 April - the Studded Wristband
20 April - 20 May - the Snake
21 May - 20 June - the Denim Patched Waistcoat
21 June - 22 July - the Spooky Pumpkin
23 July - 22 August - the Leather Jacket
23 August - 22 September - the Long Hair

23 September - 22 October - the Cannons
23 October - 21 November - the Horns
22 November - 21 December - the Bat
22 December - 19 January - the Jack Daniels
20 January - 18 February - the Cucumber
19 February - 20 March - the Skull

Ian and I are both the sign of the Skull, Jenni is the Bat.

Predictions for this week:
Studded Wristband – You might have problems with Mars this week. Maybe keep your bars in the fridge so they don't melt.
Snake – Avoid any Rue Morgues and strange lands this week. Lucky numbers are 666 and 22.
Denim Patched Waistcoat – Hoovering while wearing flares is an unwise move this week. Saturn says he might come round your house to return your Hawkwind LP but he doesn't.
Spooky Pumpkin – Cryptic writings may cause a disagreement between you and a friend, practice tolerance because Mustaine riffs in mysterious ways.
Leather Jacket – You'll be patronised by a Spice Girls fan this week who tries to tell you you'd like them if you listened to a whole album, tell them you think they are talking from Uranus.
Long Hair – Fortune favours the hairy this week and Timotei the patron saint of the shiny haired smiles upon you from a mountain stream, expect to win at least a tenner on the lottery.
Cannons – You find yourself in a situation as complex as the swirls on a Viennetta this week, don't overthink it, just go to the pub.
Horns – You'll win some and lose some this week, but that's the way you like it, Baby.

Bat – Dark clouds gather which suits you fine and is all the better for initiating bewitching dark romances. A small sacrifice of dropping goat's cheese on the floor should help matters along.
Jack Daniels - It's going to be a Mötley Crüe fifth album kind of week so you're safest spending most of it in bed.
Cucumber – This week Saturday will be your lucky bunday so be prepared for wearing or being a flesh tuxedo.
Skull – Cosmic forces align this week to make you irresistible to the opposite sex so wear your best pants and nip to Boots for some protection (and we don't mean sun cream, wink wink).

Thursday 7th August
We went to the river today. Bruce lent Jenni his portable CD player and we took this and a blanket and lay in the overgrown grass at the old swimming place (it sounds a bit Scooby-Do doesn't it, Dear Diary?). Half of it is concrete and half of it is long grass. It's not visible from the foot path because of some massive willow trees. You have to know it's there to find it and most people don't know it's there, which is just how we like it. Bruce told us about it.
Ian was in a weird mood. He made us promise we wouldn't lose touch when we finish school (which isn't for a whole year). We sunbathed, protected by trees.

Friday 8th August
We went to the river and had a boozy picnic with T-Reg, Dazza, Ella, Shot, and Lizzie. Malibu and cherryade is wonderful. It's like angels having a mosh pit on your tongue. I kept hoping Ella would suggest we played spin the bottle but she didn't. She has snogged T-Reg and Dazza already.

Saturday 9th August
Ella told me that Van Halen insist on having the brown ones taken out of the M&Ms in their dressing room. I think Dave Lee Roth is a twerp Dear Diary. One of Ella's ambitions is to get backstage at a Van Halen or Mötley Crüe concert. She flirted with the bar man and asked him why the new Crüe album isn't on the jukebox. He said he'd try and get it on there. I'm not sure it's fair for women to do this. Dazza can't flirt and get the Bathory album he wants on the jukebox.
STF said he'd been round Owen Tranter's house and Owen had challenged him to a game of soggy biscuit. Everyone said "Eeeeww!" so I did, but I don't actually know what soggy biscuit is. STF said Owen is still going out with Jessica Rice. Even though it's the summer holidays there is still plenty of gossip. Lizzie said she quite fancies the guy in HMV who wears eyeliner. Ella said it was about time she got interested in men. Shot said there is something very appealing about men who look like women. She said they seem safe and familiar, rather than alien and hairy. Mopey Dick was wearing his full length black leather jacket tonight, despite it being roasting hot in the pub. T-Reg called him Betty Swallocks.

Sunday 10th August
Mum said I can stay over at Jenni's tonight. We had tea (I mean dinner) with her Mum and Dad and her brother Bruce. It was sun dried tomato and mozzarella tartlets with Mediterranean vegetable couscous. Jenni doesn't know what soggy biscuit is. We sat outside until late. It was really peaceful.

Monday 11th August
Do you know what soggy biscuit is Dear Diary? It might just be an old people word for a type of biscuit, like when Nanny Howard's neighbour says sticky willy instead of iced bun.

Tuesday 12th August
Dilemma for Ian: If he could have sex with one of the Spice Girls but he had to listen to their album (on repeat if necessary) while he did it, would he?
Clarifying question: Can he hum very loudly? Answer, yes.
Clarifying question: Can he wear earplugs? Answer, no.
He's thinking about it.
Ian and I picked blackberries for Betty today. There are loads of them in the lane at the back of her house. She told us to pick the ones from waist height and higher because she said some people walk their dogs along the back lane so the ones from lower down might have added ingredients. While we were picking blackberries a man with an Alsatian came down the lane. The dog looked affronted to find us there so he probably was going to wee on the blackberries.
Betty gave us some Battenberg and lemonade. She told me my hair looked lovely and it was my crowning glory. Then we went to Ian's and listened to Deep Purple's Stormbringer album. I thought the song "You Can't Do It Right (With The One You Love)" was weird. If you can't do it right with the one you love, then who can you do it right with? I think David Coverdale probably has loads of women on the go at once and gets cockfuzzled* about which one he likes best. Ian decided he would have sex with Ginger Spice while humming very loudly. He'd hum Iron Maiden's "Wasted Years" because he finds that very satisfying to hum.

*Useful new word Dear Diary for describing being confused about who you like best. There is a female equivalent: fannywildered. This has happened to Ella more than once.

Wednesday 13th August

Mum says she doesn't mind me wearing with-it clothes but going out with your bra on show is added to the list of things I can't do until I'm eighteen. I told her people don't say "with it" any more. She said she meant things that are "all the rage". I said people don't say that any more either, plus I'm not wearing fashionable clothes, I'm wearing metal clothes. There is a massive and important difference (fashion clothes are shit and metal clothes rule, obviously).

All this is because I customised a White Zombie T-shirt and you can see a tiny bit of bra when I lift my arm but it's not that bad. I said it was a clean bra and I'd keep my arms by my side. She said I could keep my arms by my side on my way upstairs to change. Would Doro Pesch, Lita Ford or even the Spice Girls ever have become famous if their Mums had kept making them go upstairs and change? I despair of this small town mentality Dear Diary, I really do.

Thursday 14th August

The front page of the Reading Chronicle didn't say "Crisis Averted Due To Bra Cover-up". Madonna had her bra on show for most of the eighties. Ginger Spice wore a union jack dress that showed her big black knickers. All I was showing was a modest hint of lace, a mere glimpse.

I had dinner at Jenni's. Bruce brought his girlfriend Minty. She was wearing a Hypercolor T-shirt that changes colour when you touch it from lilac to pinky white. She had pinky white armpits throughout the evening. They don't have salad cream on their salad. They have vinaigrette dressing or balsamic vinegar.
I found out what soggy biscuit is. Minty told us. This is the most disgusting thing I've ever heard. I'm not even going to write it down properly, Dear Diary, but it's basically a game where men race to reach a happy trouser conclusion, aim the result at an innocent and yummy biscuit and then there is a terrible forfeit for the slowest to decorate the biscuit. I'm glad I'm a girl and we don't do this sort of thing.

Friday 15th August
How do you become the sort of woman men give flowers to? The Spice Girls are advertising Impulse now. Actually, I get hay fever so I would much prefer chocolates to flowers.
We went to this cool shop in Smelly Alley today. Jenni needed a new bulb for her lava lamp. It's called Graffiti and it has legal highs like guarana and bongs and UV stuff and nose studs. I don't think I'd get on very well with legal or illegal highs, I felt a bit funny just from the smell of all the incense. I think my vices are long haired men, being untidy, vodka, cider, fizzy wine and Malibu.
I got my period this evening.
Mum bought home a box of those ice lollies in the shape of feet. What a revolting idea. I don't want to eat anything in the shape of feet, who does she think I am? Sarah Ferguson?

Saturday 16th August

Ella told me tonight that I should practice on the cute boys in my year so I'm ready when actual men pay me attention. She said that's what she does. She said she has snogged T-Reg more than once (yes, Dear Diary, I am jealous even though I know it's not a very positive emotion according to Mum's magazines), and snogged Bob and Darren, plus she wanked off Owen Tranter. Owen Tranter scares me, he always looks angry, but maybe it's impossible to be angry when someone is wanking you off. Ella said T-Reg is a very good kisser.

If I had to pick someone to practice on it would be Danzig. I'm half an inch taller than him. I bet Danzig doesn't give women flowers, unless they're black ones. He's such a sex god, albeit a somewhat short and tightly packed one.

Gods list (international)
Glenn Danzig
Pete Steele
Max Cavalera
Rob Flynn
Christopher Lee
Elvira Mistress Of The Dark
Rob Zombie
Ice-T
Ingrid Pitt
Rob Newman

Sometimes my Gods list is quite Dave heavy, but this time it's overpopulated by Robs.

Gods list (Reading)
Tyrannosaurus Reg (the very good kisser)
Barry (kissing ability unknown)

Jenni's Gods list (international)
Marilyn Manson
Nick Cave
Twiggy Ramirez
Pete Steele
Johnny Depp
Kenny Hickey
Robert Smith
Dani Filth
Kat Bjelland
Shirley Manson

Jenni's Gods list (Reading)
Lex
Darren

Sunday 17th August
Dad day. We went to the Sunday market and boot sale then to Nanny Howard's. At the boot sale we saw Matty Bateman. He was looking at a computer game stall. I said hello. Dad asked me if Matty was a special friend of mine. I said no, he was generally a flatulent nuisance. Nanny Howard did a roast dinner, it was lush. She gave me some magazines for Mum, including some Cosmopolitans, which tend to have interesting bits in.

Monday 18th August
Mum moaned because I've eaten all the chocolate ice cream out of the tub of Neapolitan again. The smart thing to do would be to buy a tub of just chocolate flavour. Who even likes Neapolitan? I bet no one who reads Cosmopolitan likes Neapolitan.

Tuesday 19th August
Mum asked who I was listening to today. She's doing her taking an interest thing. There's really no need because she won't understand. I said "Manowar". She said "Menopause?" Why would there be a heavy metal band called menopause?

Wednesday 20th August
Me, Ian and Jenni went to Dawson's music shop (near the very Gothily named Abbatoirs Road, under the railway bridge, and also near RG1s nightclub which everyone at school except the metal heads wants to get into). They had no pointy guitars so Ian wasn't impressed. I looked longingly at bass guitars and even more longingly at the long haired guy behind the counter. We also went to Shakti (a sort of hippy shop that Jenni likes. It smells of incense and is not the sort of place you expect to find in Reading). Jenni bought a purple bracelet. She said the man in the shop was cute. He had dark curly hair. She said hippy types are usually very good in bed.

Thursday 21st August
We went to HMV so Jenni could get The Cramps new album then we had strawberries on the lawn at Jenni's with whipped cream and crushed up meringue and amaretti biscuits. Minty joined us to sunbathe. She is really lovely. She doesn't like metal but I can

forgive her that. She wears white trousers and sounds like she rides a horse. She was asking me and Jenni about boys today. I told her about the deliciousness that is Barry and the wonder of T-Reg. Jenni told her about luscious Lex and dazzling Dazza. Minty was telling us about when she met Bruce during freshers week but she met loads of other guys too and so they didn't start dating for a while. She is studying meteorology. University sounds terrifying if you're shy. You're in a place you've never been with people you don't know. I said this to Minty and she said that it's okay, because everyone is new and scared, like the first day of school, and it all works out just fine. She told me just to smile if I feel shy, then people will know I'm friendly and will talk to me. She said smart girls like me and Jenni should go to university. Jenni has already decided to go. I'd better wait and see how I feel, I can't even imagine GCSEs being over. No one in my family has been to university.

Friday 22nd August
This is going to be an amazing weekend Dear Diary, party tonight, pub tomorrow and festival on Monday!
STF's parents are on holiday so there's a bring your own booze party at his house tonight. It's just some people from school going and we are sworn to secrecy because STF doesn't want it to get out of hand and to get bollocked by the neighbours. His parents told him he could have a few friends to stay over but not a party so officially it's not a party (but it kind of is a party). He's invited T-Reg, Bob, Darren, Lizzie, Ella, Shot, Me, Ian and Jenni. Ian and I got some K cider from the shop on the way, Jenni took a bottle of rosé wine from her parents wine rack. She actually

asked first and it was okay! Her Mum told her she had to share it though and asked if she wanted some olives as well.

I asked Mum what time I have to be in tonight and she said 11:00 as usual. This sucks because ideally I'd be staying over at STF's. I tried unsuccessfully to negotiate a midnight and then an 11:30 curfew. I'm just going to have to try and have a load of fun before 11:00. Even Cinderella is allowed out later than me. Everything happens at midnight: see Fastway's "After Midnight", Iron Maiden's "Two Minutes To Midnight" and Judas Priest's "Living After Midnight". I bet Rob Halford's bedroom is swarming with women after midnight but at eleven o'clock it's just him in his leather hat writing lyrics.

We played spin the bottle, just kissing, not full on snogs. Girls didn't mind kissing girls but boys spun again if they landed on each other. I got kissed by Darren and STF. I had to kiss Ian and Shot. Darren explained how to wank a girl off, using the two fingers one thumb method. T-Reg said he calls this his love gun and pointed his two fingers at me while wiggling his thumb! Ian walked me home. Darren walked Jenni home.

Saturday 23rd August

Last night Ian almost did it! He and Ella ended up being the only ones still awake and she said she would do it with him if he had a condom. They snogged and he felt her boobs (outside bra). He said she was drunker than he'd ever seen her and he could never take advantage of a drunk woman. Also, he didn't have a condom, but even if he had he said he would have waited for her to sober up before doing anything below the waist. Ian is such a diamond among men. Jenni was disturbed saying goodnight to

Dazza by her Mum. Pam invited him to come in. He did but went a bit shy. Pam said she prefers to know Jenni's friends.
Tonight me, Jenni and Ian went to the Green Man with Bob, Shot, STF and T-Reg. Shot told me in the toilets tonight that Ella thinks she's fat and worries about her weight and if boys fancy her. I couldn't believe this, boys definitely fancy her. Ella's not fat, she's a bit bigger than me but she's taller and older and she has amazing boobs, I'd say they are probably a C cup (Ian could supply more information!) Shot is probably a B. Ella is pretty but Shot is beautiful.

Sunday 24th August
Finally Dear Diary I am actually going to a gig instead of just reading about them in Metal Hammer and Kerrang! I was ready to go to the festival early. I wore denim cut offs (Mum has relented and suspended her no shorts rule due to the hot weather and due to the original rule being stupid) with a Slayer patch on one side of my bottom plus a Metallica Creeping Death patch on the other side, black shiny tights, my Nine Inch Nails vest and a red and black check shirt. I wore my 14 hole DMs, sunglasses and Misfits baseball cap. I kept looking at my ticket and reading: Reading Festival Day Ticket Sunday 24th August 1997. I still almost can't believe Mum agreed to let me go, but Dad paid for the ticket, I don't have to be up for school the next day, it's local and Jenni's brother Bruce, who is an adult, is taking us so she ran out of reasons to object.

    Roy dropped us off by RG1s and we walked to the festival site. I have never seen so many Goths in one place. In fact I've never seen so many people in one place. When we got near the festival, all the local shops (except the fancy dress shop) had people outside selling cans of beer. We had to queue for ages to swop our tickets for wristbands to get into the arena. We wandered around for a bit and then saw the Descendents. They made me think of Shot, she'd have liked them. I liked them. During 3 Colours Red we went to get a drink and went to the loo. The loos were horrible but I'd been expecting that. Next we saw Dinosaur Jr. Bruce loves them, I think "Freak Scene" is a cool song but I don't know anything else by them. They were good live Dear Diary. We got some chips (three pounds with an extra fifty pee for ketchup or mayonnaise!) and sat on the grass for a while.

   Marilyn Manson was on next and all the Goths assembled by the stage. Marilyn Manson was awesome and I don't think he has stolen Alice Cooper's act. I got goosebumps when he sang "Sweet Dreams". We went for a look at the stalls during Bush. Terrorvision were happy and bouncy. Then it was time for Metallica. They played some of their early stuff (Creeping Death, Battery, For Whom The Bell Tolls) and some covers (So What and Last Caresse). Dear Diary, until you have stood in a field on a sunny afternoon with your best friends and heard Metallica play "Nothing Else Matters" you have not felt true happiness. Metallica chucked loads of metallic confetti all over the field at the end of their set. It was like a blizzard. I caught a bit and am going to keep it forever. I couldn't quite believe it when it was over because I didn't want it to be.

Jenni borrowed money from Bruce to get a Marilyn Manson Long Sleeve T-shirt. The back print says "I am the god of fuck". Mum would go mental if I attempted to wear this. We met Jenni's Dad on the industrial estate behind the festival and he drove us all home because it was late. We said thanks to Bruce for taking us and thanks to Roy for giving us a lift home.

Monday 25th August
I'm still wearing my festival wristband. I'm not taking it off. It reminds me that some days are amazing days. I'd have loved to be old enough to have gone to Reading Festival when it was rock and metal on all three days, not just squashed onto the Sunday. Alice Cooper and Zodiac Mindwarp and the Sisters Of Mercy have all played Reading Festival before. It was on the news today that there were some drug arrests at the festival and Mum got all worked up. There are always drug arrests at the festival. I smelt a smell which I know to be weed a few times (we have a small gaggle of stoners at school, who tend to smoke behind the Maths block with us) but no one tried to sell me drugs in an organised way, but there were a few people walking through the crowd shouting the names of the drugs they had for sale. I reassured Mum that I had nothing stronger than a cider. She doesn't mind me drinking a little bit. She likes a Baileys or a Tia Maria or a port and lemon, or an anything really at Christmas and special occasions.

Tuesday 26th August
Ian and I went to see Betty. We had lemonade and Mr Kipling Bakewell slices. We told her about the festival. She said she'd seen it on the telly. She said when she was our age she used to love going roller skating at the Corn Exchange.
Mrs Butler called round with some magazines for Mum. She also bought us a marrow, spare from her garden. I hope Mum doesn't cook it, we don't really like it. When Mum came home and saw the marrow she frowned. She hates wasting stuff.

Wednesday 27th August

Jon Bon Jovi is number one. Ella and Lizzie are pleased. Me, Ian and Jenni met them and Bob and T-Reg in the park. Ella was wearing a really low cut top. I hope I become an area of outstanding natural boobies soon.

Mum made stuffed marrow for dinner. There were a lot of leftovers. I find marrow to be more of a texture than a taste.

Thursday 28th August

There's a new Oasis album out, excuse me while I don't rush to HMV and wet my pants in excitement.

Jenni's Dad (sorry Roy, he always tells me to call him Roy, but it sounds weird) was talking about the Spice Girls today. He was saying they are a hollow kind of feminism. He thinks there should be one whose "personality" is based on intelligence. Perhaps Smarty Spice or Boffin Spice. I had dinner at Jenni's. We had cheese and leek sausages, onion gravy and sweet potato mash, which is orange. It was nicer than stuffed marrow.

Friday 29th August

There is still three-quarters of a stuffed marrow in the fridge. The only good marrow is Tracy Marrow.

Ian decided he needs some condoms. We went to look in Boots but didn't buy any.

Saturday 30th August

Ian said "He's got unprotected armadillos in his pants, it's really quite frightening". Me, Ian and Jenni went to Superdrug and looked at condoms but he didn't buy any. He's going to buy some from the machine in the pub loos.

Everyone in the year above us got their GCSE results this week. No one I know failed. Dazza did better than he expected, Ella did worse than she expected. Ella told me it's boring to hear me going on about T-Reg and if I like him I should just tell him and then snog him. Shot told her not to be mean and said I'd tell him in my own time and in my own way. Yeah, thanks Shot, I will, just as soon as I work out my own way. Ian had a successful mission to the gents and is now ready to rubber up, Dear Diary, at the next available opportunity.

Sunday 31st August
Princess Diana and Dodi Al-Fayed are dead! They were killed in a car crash. It's on the front page of every newspaper and on the news. Nanny Howard said it was a tragedy. She said she thought Diana had the happiest years of her life ahead of her now she's not in an unhappy marriage but now those years have been cut short. She said she feels so sorry for the two young princes, growing up without their Mum to guide them. We all went a bit quiet, no-one knew what to say.
Today has been a weird day and tomorrow it's back to school. Dad asked how school was going and asked me if I needed anything. He said I'm smart, like his side of the family. When we left Nanny Howard's I asked if his bedsit was nice. He said it was small but he liked it and that living with Nanny Howard would drive him mad. He said he'll take me to see where he lives if I like. He always takes me to see Nanny Howard because it makes her day he says. I don't know if I'm sad or happy today.

September

Monday 1st September
Back to school. I changed at Ian's as usual. While I was taking my top off (he always turns his back, Dear Diary because he is a) a gentleman, b) not interested since he's had a hold of Ella's more massive ones) I thought about what Ella had said about practising on boys in my year. I could never do this, it would be dishonest. I also thought about what Nanny Howard said about Princess Diana no longer being in an unhappy marriage. Mum and Dad are also no longer in an unhappy marriage but they don't seem to be loads happier.
I walked past some thirteen year olds today and they were talking about forming a Spice Girls based gang and arguing about who would be who. I hate to see young minds being poisoned by rubbish music.
I am now in my GCSE exams school year which everyone keeps going on about. Your future job prospects...blah blah blah...your opportunity to make the best of yourselves (already doing that with a Wonderbra thanks)...your passport to a successful adult life...the door to a potentially glittering future and so on. T-Reg and Bob have left school. T-Reg is being a sparky (electrician) and Bob is in an office. I am now very unlikely to ever see T-Reg in shorts, unless he wins the lottery and begs me to accompany him on a luxury cruise to a tropical island where we'll drink Malibu and cherryade out of coconuts and make love on the beach while the sun sets upon his perfect and gently bobbing bottom (sorry Dear Diary, I may have got a bit carried away there, today has been a rather dull day and my brain is trying to inject some glamour into your pages). STF, Darren, Ella, Lizzie and Shot are all

in the sixth form. Lex and Mopey are in their last year of A level. We will now only see T-Reg and Bob in the Green Man.
We started Brave New World in English. Today feels a bit like the start of something new. Also, I have a new pencil case, with nothing written on it yet. Brave New World is about a future society. Some women are freemartins, meaning they aren't fertile so don't have to bother with contraception. This sounds good. Ian wanted to know why they use a card index for storing information when we have computers. Miss Wallace pointed out that there weren't computers when the book was written. Jenni asked Miss Wallace questions about Bokanovsky's Process and wanted to know how close we are to being able to do this, since Dolly the sheep was a success.

Tuesday 2nd September
In Humanities we answered the question is Heavy Metal a religion? Mrs Rogers is clearly trying to engage us by making the subject relevant. We humoured her, since she was trying her best. Jenni did most of the talking. She said yes, it is and no, it isn't. It has the good aspects of a religion (shared identity, shared values, activities, particular clothes to wear) but not the bad aspects (intolerance and unquestioning acceptance of nonsense someone else told you to think).

Wednesday 3rd September
We're doing woodwork in CDT. Who needs woodwork? All our furniture is from the second hand shop near Nanny Howard's house and it's full of stuff from floor to ceiling so no one needs to make more furniture. We aren't making anything useful in woodwork. We have the choice between making an owl with slot

in wings or a small CD rack (I already have a plastic one). I'm making an owl. I've noticed we never get to do the T (technology) in CDT. I was hoping to make a robot vacuum cleaner like Mum got excited about when it was on Tomorrow's World. Mr Askew's GCSE pep talk was a lot less peppy than all the previous ones teachers have given us this week. He said some of us will end up doing boring jobs for little money and so we'd better pull our fingers out.

I used to sometimes see T-Reg on the way to CDT and I still look for him but then I remember that he is now a working man.

Poem for T-Reg:

Tyrannosaurus Reg, you left,
Before my love was fully fledged
Now you're a nine to five sparky
And I'm still here, darkly
It's only on Satyrday* night
I might glimpse you
Irresistible, I should know better,
You're a weekend treat like Viennetta.

Ian, Gav and I watched some WWE wrestling round Ian's. The Undertaker is quite fit. Ian was telling me it looks like wrestlers have got small dicks but it's just because the rest of them is so muscular.

*This is a clever play on words Dear Diary. The sort of people who laugh at the jokes in Shakespeare will get it.

Thursday 4th September

In Brave New World everyone belongs to everyone else and there aren't families. People can have sex with who they like and no-one calls anyone a slag, in fact if you don't sleep around you're weird. This world would suit Ella and Mark Dobbs but not Lizzie. I haven't decided if it would suit me yet, plus the clothes sound a bit awful in Brave New World.

I had some crisps made out of vegetables at Jenni's. Not normal potato crisps, they were made out of parsnips, beetroot and carrot. As Nanny Howard would say "Well, that's news to me". Mum came home from work with a bag of clothes that one of the women she worked with thought I might like. Her daughter is going to university and was having a sort out. There were dungarees, ugh! Some jeans that are too big for me right now, a sweatshirt with Minnie Mouse on (I am fifteen!), and a sundress with a sun, moon and star print that's actually quite nice. I asked Mum if we're officially poor. She said we're not as well off as when Dad lived with us but we're not too bad. I wanted to ask if she feels that her happiest years are ahead of her now that she's no longer in an unhappy marriage but I think the answer is no.

Friday 5th September

We set fire to a peanut again in Biology. I swear I've done this three times now Dear Diary, I get it, heat is a kind of energy, and peanuts have got energy in them. We told the supply teacher we'd done it but they said we were going to do it again and then they also set fire to some lettuce (best thing to do with it, who likes lettuce?). Peanuts are going to think I've got something personal against them, but I haven't, some of my best times have included peanuts (Christmas, pub, parties).

Saturday 6th September
Today is the funeral of Princess Diana. There is nothing much else on the telly. The Green Man was awful tonight. We got invaded by Carina Norman! She and Janine came in with two boys I don't know. Carina said Hi and gave me the lightest and falsest hug I've ever had (I returned it with an equally false one). It might be best in future to just hiss at each other and try and look big. They left after about half an hour but somehow left a lingering taint. Mopey Dick is drinking Pernod and black. You don't pronounce the "d", Dear Diary (in Pernod, I mean, you do pronounce it in Dick, otherwise he'd be called Mopey Ick).

Sunday 7th September
I had a lie in and watched my Jo Brand video. I had a big think about feminism. I am a partial feminist Dear Diary. Jenni's Dad assumes I'm a feminist, which in itself is him imposing his views on women). I think that women should get paid as much as men for the same jobs, and should do the same amount of housework and should be as free to have sex with as many people as they want but I don't mind wearing a bra and trying to look attractive to men because it's fun and I want to be attractive to men. Men have loads to gain from feminism too, but they don't realise it because they think it's run by short haired women in trousers that want to stop you from seeing Barbara Windsor's bosom (like in Carry On Girls).

Monday 8th September
Carina Norman asked me and Jenni if we enjoyed the pub on Saturday. Jenni didn't reply. Carina said it was a freak show and

she won't be going again, she said she has got a better pub to go to where they have Robbie Williams and Peter Andre on the jukebox. This suits me fine. Having to put up with her Monday to Friday is more than enough to try the patience of a saint.
Mark Dobbs is a dickhead. He called Donna Harlow "Flora" because he said he's heard she spreads easily. He's such a hypocrite. He is the perviest boy in our year, why can't Donna be equally active? This is supposed to be the nineties and we've got ladette culture, but in most people's heads it's still the fifties. In Brave New World Helmholtz Watson is said to have had six hundred and forty girls in less than four years. This makes him the Gene Simmons of Brave New World. Bernard Marx reminds me of Mopey Dick a bit.

Tuesday 9th September
I hate ladette culture. It's far, far better to go quietly about your business doing what you want rather than shrieking about the place flashing your boobs with one hand and drinking a can of lager with the other. When this sort of thing is on the telly it makes Mum twitchy about letting me go out at the weekend.

Wednesday 10th September
Trent Reznor is looking smoking hot on the cover of Kerrang! this week. Jenni is going to need new pants after this one. Me and Ian saw a rainbow so we took it as a sign to listen to Gav's Rainbow and Dio records. My fave tracks were "Dream Evil" and "All Night Long".

Thursday 11th September
Janine Sackett had to read an embarrassing bit of Brave New World in English today. Bernard goes to an orgy (called a solidarity service). One of the characters in the book had an eyebrow like Barry's which I thought was odd because all the other little problems seem to have been sorted out in the Brave New World. Surely if they can make clones and cure senility they can stop people having megabrows?
I had dinner at Jenni's. It was boeuf bourguignon, which is just beef stew Dear Diary. If I say it fast and don't think about it I can say it properly but if I look at it written down I struggle with it.

Friday 12th September
I have grown! Today me and Jenni went to C&A and I stood by the giraffe height chart in the children's department, like I always do. She grew off the top of the chart last year. I am now five foot, three and a half inches tall. I'm taller than Danzig by half an inch. I am still a 32A bra though.
Me, Ian, Jenni and Matty went to the cinema tonight to see Austin Powers: International Man Of Mystery. It was pretty funny and I liked the clothes. Matty sat by Ian and tried to be normal. Actually Dear Diary, out of school, when he's not trying to impress people by lighting his farts, he's okay. Like me and Ian he's read loads of Terry Pratchett books. He also reads the same Ravenloft vampire books that Jenni loves.

Saturday 13th September
Shot was wearing an X-Ray Spex T-Shirt tonight. She bought it in Camden. She was telling us what a great place it is to go shopping. She also went to Kensington Market which has a goth

shop called The Black Rose with changing rooms decorated to look like coffins! Jenni and I really want to go.

Ella joked that she'd lost her virginity but she still had the box it came in. She was chatting up the barman all night.

Sunday 14th September

Hooray! It's Dad day today. I told him all about Reading Festival and showed him my wristband. Nanny Howard said she had seen it on the news but she didn't spot me. She pronounced Metallica as "Metal Licker!" Bless her, she tries to understand the stuff I like but always gets it sort of wrong.

Something amazing happened when Dad took me home. Mum invited him in for a cup of tea. We all sat in the living room together for the first time since the day he left. The conversation was mostly about me but I suppose this is a safe topic.

Monday 15th September

In Brave New World everyone is happy and if they aren't they take a drug called soma. The character Lenina says "Everybody's happy nowadays" which made me think of the Buzzcocks song and she says "Never put off till tomorrow the fun you can have today". I think she'd be good to go to the pub with but I bet she'd sleep with T-Reg.

Mark Dobbs read out a letter from Penthouse magazine. A woman had dipped her boyfriend's youknowwhat in strawberry yogurt and basically used it as a spoon. I prefer black cherry yogurt and sometimes I like to dip a custard cream in my yogurt. There are loads of new flavours of Müller yogurt all the time but so far thankfully not penis flavour.

Tuesday 16th September

Everyone at school is saying "Groovy, Baby!" because of Austin Powers: International Man Of Mystery. When Weebles announced that we had no German homework he was met with a small chorus of "Groovy, Baby!" He looked really puzzled. I bet he only watches boring films with subtitles.

I've gone off yogurt. Jenni said you shouldn't be putting penises in it because of the natural bacteria. I don't want to eat bacteria, even if it is cherry flavoured. Also, this is information I just don't need Dear Diary, it's very unlikely to come up in a GCSE exam.

Wednesday 17th September

Ian and I went to see Betty after school. She gave us lemonade and a Dairy Crunch bar each. She asked us how school was going. Ian told her we are studying for our GCSEs now. Gav did really well in his and Betty has promised him some money if he does well but told him it's not the be all and end all and that different people are good at different things and we can't all be Clive Sinclair. She left school at fourteen. She worked in a factory until she got married and said it was hard work but they had a giggle. They used to go to the Majestic Ball Room when they got paid on a Friday.

Thursday 18th September

The Prodigy are in trouble because of "Smack My Bitch Up", apparently it encourages violence towards women. I bet Cannibal Corpse are going to keep a low profile, they've written way worse stuff than this. I don't think you're meant to take this stuff seriously, it's like horror films and Alice Cooper's stage show, it's just entertainment.

Friday 19th September
Carina dared Janine to push Charmaine down the stairs today. Janine gave her a few little shoves then Charmaine refused to walk in front of Janine or Carina. Carina looked annoyed. She is such a ball of spite Dear Diary. Betty tells me that "If you can't say anything nice don't say anything at all", but clearly no one has ever told Carina this. If there was a GCSE in being the spawn of Satan she'd get an A* because she's already done all the coursework.

Saturday 20th September
Today is the worst day of my life. When I got in from the pub Mum was still up and she told me that Dad had died. Uncle Brian went round to see him this morning and he didn't answer so he got worried. He got the spare key from the next door neighbour and found Dad in bed, not breathing, not alive. He had been dead for hours and he couldn't be resuscitated.

Sunday 21st September
I don't even really remember writing yesterday's entry. I don't think I can write anything much today because nothing makes sense or seems important right now. Mum told me that Dad probably died of a massive heart attack (like Grandad Howard did) and would have died in his sleep and not been in pain. She told me this is a thought we have to take comfort from. She asked me if I wanted to see Dad's body. Right now it's in the chapel of rest. I said no.

Monday 22nd September
Mum said I didn't have to go to school today so I didn't. Ian and Jenni came round after school. We don't usually hang out at my house unless Mum is at work but she let them come round and let us go up to my room for a bit.

Tuesday 23rd September
Gutted doesn't even begin to cover how I feel. Uncle Brian is arranging the funeral. I'm mostly staying upstairs in my room.

Wednesday 24th September
Mum suggested I go out to get some fresh air. I went to WH Smiths and got Kerrang! Then I came straight home. I didn't really want to talk to anyone. This week there's a poster of Max Cavalera and some stuff about Hole who I sort of like. Courtney Love seems sort of mad. Maybe she's gone off her head since Kurt died.

Thursday 25th September
Dad's funeral is arranged for Tuesday. His cause of death is confirmed as a heart attack.

Friday 26th September
I cleaned Mustaine out. As usual he only swam in a tiny area of the bath tub. Mum let me order Dominos pizza for tea.

Saturday 27th September
I went to the pub with Jenni and Ian. I didn't tell anyone about Dad. Some idiot put loads of Limp Bizkit on the jukebox. I don't want to listen to "music" made by someone who doesn't know

how to operate a hat. Also Limp Bizkit is the grimmest name ever, it's a really lazy attempt to be shocking, with one percent of the effort that Alice Cooper or Marilyn Manson puts in.

Sunday 28th September

It's a bit like life has stopped. Mum says we need to get the funeral over but I don't see how this will change anything. I read some Brave New World because I don't want to get too behind and also it's a good book. In Brave New World they don't get sad about death: "the social body persists although the component cells may change". The trouble is, I'm not in Brave New World and I loved the component cells of my Dad. I could do with some soma. It stops you thinking about the past or the future.

Monday 29th September

Tuesday 30th September

Dad's Funeral.
Mum woke me up at eight and told me to get dressed and have breakfast. She told me I could wear whatever I wanted. I sort of knew not to push it and wore my Slayer T-shirt under a black jumper with a long black skirt. I'm a bit worried Mum is going mad. She told me she dreamt of Dad last night. When we got to the crematorium Mum and Nanny Howard hugged each other for a long time. They haven't actually spoken for about a year and a half, although they have exchanged magazines.
I don't know what to say to anyone and no one knows what to say to me. Ian and his Dad came to the funeral, and Jenni and her parents. It all felt real but not real, like I was watching a film, and I wanted to talk to people but I couldn't talk to them. The worst bit

of the whole day, the bit I will never, ever forget, even if I live to be one hundred, was when the coffin disappeared behind the curtains. Mum was crying on one side of me and Nanny Howard was crying on the other side of me.
Uncle Brian read a poem:

Do Not Stand At My Grave And Weep - Mary Elizabeth Frye

Do not stand at my grave and weep,
I am not there, I do not sleep,
I am a thousand winds that blow
I am the diamond glints on snow
I am the sunlight on ripened grain
I am the gentle Autumn rain

When you awaken in the morning's hush
I am the swift uplifting rush
Of quiet birds in circled flight
I am the soft stars that shine at night
Do not stand at my grave and cry
I am not there, I did not die

Dad isn't having a gravestone. Ages ago, when his Dad (my Grandad Howard) died, he told Uncle Brian that when he dies he just wants to be scattered in the rose garden at the crematorium. It's hard for atheists to decide stuff like this.

October

Wednesday 1st October

I went back to school today. Everyone is being really nice to me, even people who are usually bell ends. None of the teachers are nagging me for any homework. All the niceness is just reminding me of the fucking huge horribleness of not having a Dad any more. Also, I don't want to become known as that sad girl whose Dad is dead. I don't know what to do right now Dear Diary, everything feels weird. I think I just have to carry on as normal but nothing feels normal and nothing normal matters to me right now.

I read up to where the class is in Brave New World this evening. There is a bit where children go to the hospital where people die so they don't get scared of death. No one would write a diary in Brave New World because they are encouraged to spend all their time with other people. At the start of the book I thought it was a good place to live but I've changed my mind.

I listened to Faster Pussycat's "No Room for Emotion". I know they are glam but Taime hits the nail on the head; "I've got no, I've got no room for emotion, It's like a cloud dripping radiation right on my head". It's from a mix tape that Lizzie made for me and gave me today. She hasn't put any Bon Jovi on it. She said she wanted to do something nice for me.

Thursday 2nd October

I didn't want to get out of bed today. I felt like if I stayed here and didn't see anyone or do anything then nothing could go wrong. Mum came in and asked me if I was ill. I said no. I was late to Ian's and had to change really fast. He hummed the Benny Hill music while I changed. I'm not sure why. He's strange but adorable.

Friday 3rd October
When I got home from school I could see Mum had been crying. She pretended to be okay. I had just ice cream for tea and Mum didn't moan. Have all the rules changed now?

Saturday 4th October
I left to go to the pub just as Blind Date was starting. None of the men on offer had long hair. When I got to the Green Man loads of the men had long hair. There were so many hotties Dear Diary, including T-Reg. I think it's true that you don't know what you've got 'til it's gone, as Cinderella sang. School is duller now he's not there. I sat next to him for most of the evening. Just smelling him makes me smile. He said I'll ace my GCSEs and so will Ian and Jenni because we turn up and we're smart. He said the teachers don't want anyone to fail, because it makes them look like bad teachers. He worked in a house this week where the woman had left her naughty knickers on the bed so he could see them and she made him and his boss a cup of tea and Boasters biscuits. I haven't even given him a biscuit, let alone shown him my knickers. Mopey Dick said the charms of an older woman are manifold.

Sunday 5th October
Manifold just means numerous or varied Dear Diary. I watched my Red Dwarf videos. Poor Lister, it must be rubbish being the last human but he is having more fun than Ann Burden did in Z For Zachariah. I got up and did some English coursework because

I didn't want to think about nuclear war. My brain seems to get stuck on topics at the moment Dear Diary, I have one troubling thought and then it hangs around for ages if I don't try and squash it.

Mum said Dad would be proud of me, beavering away at my homework. She has started talking about him a lot. She never used to mention him. Since I heard Pop Will Eat Itself's "Beaver Patrol" I no longer think of big toothed mammals when I hear beaver. It's Mrs Slocombe's pussy all over again. I have a badge which says "I'm a Butlin's Beaver" which I'll probably never wear but will keep forever to remind me what it's like to have a happy family.

Monday 6th October

Brave New World has now got Shakespeare in it. There is a savage who is not part of the Brave New World and he has read all of Shakespeare. I like that in Brave New World contraception is all sorted out and babies are grown outside women's bodies and having sex is just a pleasant activity. We could do with some of these ideas being reality right now (the bit about deciding people's social class and abilities before birth is maybe a bit troubling, but not much more so than when they split us into separate Maths groups based on ability at the start of school). Mum has stopped making me come straight home on Mondays and Fridays. I tell her I'm going to the library to do my homework sometimes (and sometimes I do go to the library), other times I hang around in town or walk in the park. Today I went into town with Shot. She needed some safety pins for a T-shirt she's customising. She said you can't buy decent punk clothes anywhere in Reading. She said when she's eighteen she's going to go out in London wearing just black masking tape over her nipples, like Wendy O Williams. She said Wendy O Williams gets misunderstood and what she does is not about sex, but is really about power.

I had cherry pie filling out of the tin for tea. I got my period today. I've just looked back and I didn't even have a period in September. Everything about that month was wrong and screwed up.

Tuesday 7th October

Donna Harlow told me she thinks she might be pregnant. All of my reading of problem pages has paid off. I know exactly what she should do. I told her she has to do a test as soon as possible. This is not one of those problems that will get better if you leave it. She said she can't afford to buy one. Her options are a) borrow the money to buy one, b) steal one, c) go to her family doctor (she won't do this, her Mum would go abso-batshit-apeshit-lutely mental crazy if she found out, she goes to church every week and thinks all sorts of stuff is a sin and doing it most definitely is. I gave Donna the fifty-seven pence I had on me.

Wednesday 8th October

Donna's cousin has bought her a test. She's going to do it tomorrow morning. Ian came round after school. We didn't bother with Kerrang! this week because there was too much Green Day. Shot hates Green Day. She says they are punk-lite and commercially appealing drivel. Mum was at work until eight. We had chicken and mushroom pot noodle and listened to Machine Head.

Thursday 9th October

Donna is not pregnant. She said she is going to be really careful from now on and as soon as she's sixteen (next month) she's going to go on the pill. I asked her what it's like having sex. She said it's rubbish at first and it hurts a bit then it gets better and then you want to do it all the time. Her boyfriend isn't at our school. He usually uses a condom but once he didn't have any so he said he'd pull out and he forgot he wasn't wearing one and didn't pull out, leading to Donna fearing she was pregnant.
Brave New World has now got too much Shakespeare in. The savage has gone a bit bonkers because of all the Shakespeare in his head and he's called the girl he loves a whore. I know what it's like to be driven mad by Shakespeare becuase we had two essays on Macbeth to do last term.

Friday 10th October

I watched Ben Elton on telly tonight. He gets very worked up about trains. The last train I went on was actually really brilliant but it was years ago and we were going on holiday to Butlins. I got a chocolate bar from a machine on the platform. I can still remember the noise the machine made when you pulled out the drawer of the chocolate bar you wanted.

Saturday 11th October

Mum said some of my pants were getting tatty so she gave me some money to buy some more. Me and Jenni went to C&A and I got some red lace ones and some black lace ones. You can sort of see my pubes through them! Mum made a really strange face when I showed them her. She said she thought I was going to get some cotton ones, like the ones that have got tatty. I wore my new pants to the pub.

Shot looked amazing tonight. She was wearing a customised Dr and the Crippens T-shirt, a leather skirt and lime green fishnet tights. Bob said he'd love to get caught in Shot's fishnets. She said she prefers men not boys! Wendy O Williams dated Lemmy and I bet if he'd been in the Green Man tonight Lemmy would have fancied Shot.

Dazza said Goths and black metal heads are compatible but black metal heads and Bon Jovi fans are not (although I happen to know he has snogged Ella). Ella wasn't out tonight. She has a date with the cute guy who works in HMV and wears nail varnish and eyeliner.

Sunday 12th October

I've swapped tatty pants for tarty pants. Hooray! The thing I like best about writing a diary is that if you think of something clever to say the day after you can say it, whereas in real life you can't. I walked through Prospect Park and under the big oaks. It felt very calm and still underneath the canopy of the huge old trees. I had Type O Negative's October Rust album on my Walkman.

I wish I could have a normal Sunday with Dad but that's gone forever now.

Monday 13th October

In Brave New World there is no senility which would be great for Nanny Brooks. Also, most people aren't individuals (like at our school when everyone wears the same top from Miss Selfridge) and those that are stubbornly individual get sent to an island.

This could be a great place but there is no heavy metal in Brave New World. Our homework is to finish reading the book. English homework doesn't always feel like homework to me and this is one of those times.

Jenni, Ian, Matty Bateman and I went to the fair in Prospect Park. We went on the ghost train and had some candy floss. We saw loads of people from school. Charmaine Payne asked Ian to go on the big wheel with him. He said he didn't like heights so Matty went on with her.

Tuesday 14th October
We went to the fair again. I wish we hadn't because we saw T-Reg and he was holding hands with a girl. He said hello to us but didn't introduce us to his companion. Ian tried to cheer me up with some fruit nougat. When I was on my own this evening I thought about something the vicar said at Dad's funeral. He said "We're born into sin and we die into sin". That is bollocks, don't blame me for stuff I haven't done. I have enough trouble with Mum at the moment. She is alright one day and then really arsey the next. I finished Brave New World and it ended with the savage killing himself. I wanted him and Lenina to have sex but they didn't.

Wednesday 15th October
When I heard Concorde fly over today I wished I could just fly off somewhere. One day Dear Diary, it's going to be me on that plane, going somewhere exciting very fast. I've never flown anywhere but it looks amazing. Maybe if I do well in my A levels (yes, I know I have to get through my GCSEs first) I could become

cabin crew on Concorde. Minty said she thought of doing this but decided to go to university instead.

Gods list (international)
Glenn Danzig
Pete Steele
Christopher Lee
Dave Lister
Rob Zombie
Dave Mustaine
Elvira Mistress Of The Dark
Rob Newman
Barry Thompson
Tank Girl

Jonathon Davies is sort of fit but maybe only because he looks like Rob Newman who I have fancied absolutely forever?

Gods list (Reading)
T-Reg
Barry

Jenni's Gods list (international)
Robert Smith
Andrew Eldritch
Trent Reznor
Pete Steele
Kenny Hickey
Johnny Depp
Kiefer Sutherland

Marilyn Manson
Tommy Lee
Nick Cave

Jenni's Gods list (Reading)
Lex
Dazza

Thursday 16th October
We did a weird thing in English today. Miss Wallace told us to write where we'll be in one, two, five, ten and twenty years. How am I meant to know? I don't even know what's going to happen tomorrow, I'm not Mystic Meg. This is what I wrote Dear Diary:

In one year I'll be sixteen. I will be old enough to legally leave school, to leave home, to buy cigarettes and to have sexual intercourse. I hope I'll have seen Alice Cooper in concert and been close enough to the stage to be covered in fake blood.

In two years I'll be doing A levels. I want to take English Literature, Sociology (probably, it's what Jenni's Dad teaches and it sounds okay but I haven't done any of it yet) and Psychology (which is lots of writing essays). I will be almost old enough to buy alcohol.

In five years I'll be working in a shop like my Mum does probably and I'll have left home.

In ten years I'll probably be married and have children.

In twenty years I don't know.

I will be thirty-five years old in twenty years, almost as old as Mum is now. She often says her life didn't work out how she expected it to. I'm not sure that I want to get married. I'm not sure that I want to work in a shop. I do like the idea of working in WH Smiths or in Thorntons though. The only things I'm sure about are that I want to see Alice Cooper and I almost definitely want to have sex (but it has to be with someone worth it).

Friday 17th October
Some bits of school are easy Dear Diary, like Textiles or English or ignoring the nonsense that Carina Norman comes out with, but some things like Maths are much harder. I hope I don't fail Maths because it would be embarrassing, but I'm not sure it'll affect my future career because a) I don't know what my future career is, b) I'm very unlikely to pick a career that has loads of Maths in. Jenni told me today that there is some Maths in Psychology called statistics.
Mum bought me a Curly Wurly.

Saturday 18th October
Mustaine is dead. I cried. That goldfish has taken some of my deepest darkest secrets to his watery grave. I hope goldfish heaven is full of lush plants and loads of friendly fishes to swim about with. I've just remembered I don't believe in heaven. Where is my Dad?
I went to the pub to drown my sorrows (two Malibu and Diet Cokes) and something brilliant happened. I saw Barry and he asked me if I wanted a drink sometime, just me and him! He

asked me for my number and gave me his number! We arranged to meet on Friday night!

Sunday 19th October
I spent all day wondering what to wear on Friday. I want to look sexy but not like I do it on first dates.

Monday 20th October
Today I feel angry and horny. Bruce Dickinson and David Baddiel were on Never Mind The Buzzcocks tonight.

Tuesday 21st October
Mark Dobbs had a copy of Mayfair today in Maths. It had the word "bazoomas" on the cover. It's a pleasant sounding word, I like the "zoom" bit in the middle. I feel really anxious today, like someone else I love is going to die. I know that's stupid, but I just feel scared. I'm trying to distract myself. I wish I was somewhere cool, like at the Whiskey a Go Go, drinking with JD with Lemmy, instead of stuck in Reading where mainly bad stuff or dull stuff happens (with the exception of Barry of course, except he hasn't happened yet, but he will on Friday. I can't believe I have his phone number, technically I could just ring him up and say hello).

Wednesday 22nd October
Ian and I went to see Betty on the way home from school. She asked me how I was feeling. This is the first time I've seen her since Dad died. I started to say "I'm very well thank you, how are you?" But I just started crying. She hugged me for ages and told Ian to make us a cup of tea. She said when she lost her Alf it broke her heart. She told me the sadness would always be there,

but little by little, each day would get easier. She told me to come round any time I wanted a shoulder to cry on or a cuddle.

Thursday 23rd October
Carina Norman was trying to get the girls in our class to admit if they had ever done a blow job today. No one would say because they knew full well if they said yes they'd be branded a slag and if they said no they'd be called frigid. She gave up asking me fairly quickly because she got no reaction at all, I just pretended not to hear her. Donna Harlow asked her if she had and she said she'd say after someone else did. Jenni said "Always a follower, never a leader". Carina asked Jenni if she ever had and Jenni said it was none of Carina's business. Matty Bateman lent me his 2000AD to read in Maths.
I had a new fruit today at Jenni's. It was called a physalis. It looked better than it tasted.

Friday 24th October
I met Barry after school. It was great apart from at the start. I think he thinks I'm in the sixth form. I think he sort of assumed I am because he's seen me in the pub and I didn't say anything because I didn't know what to say. If I told him I wasn't he might think I was telling him in case he was going to have sex with me tonight and then I'd look arrogant, like I think he would obviously want to have sex with me. Also, we were in a pub and the bar man was nearby so I couldn't say I was fifteen. He took me to a quieter pub than the Green Man so we could talk. I had thought about all sorts of potentially awkward conversational stuff Dear Diary, like suppose he says he likes a shit band or suppose he asks me if he can come in when he walks me home, but I wasn't

prepared for this. I also didn't tell him about my Dad. I already feel like I've got a big Rob Zombie style cross on my head at school, marking me out as that girl with the dead dad that might go mental. I found out that my teacher had told the whole class what had happened when I had a week off.
The pub he took me to for a drink was lovely. It had leather chairs and a chandelier. There was hand cream in the toilet. I had a vodka and lime (a bit more mature than a Malibu and Diet Coke I thought, Dear Diary). I let him do most of the talking; he told me about the people he works with, about his Mum (his parents are separated but he sees his Dad still. I told him my parents were separated but didn't elaborate), and about his plans to eventually do up houses and rent them out. After we'd been talking for a few hours he kissed me! On the mouth! He tasted of lager and Embassy No. 1. Apart from me being my stupidly shy self I had a great time. He kissed me again by the massive hedge up the road and said he'd take me for a drink again. He's going to ring me on Wednesday.

Saturday 25th October
Jenni asked me if I was still in possession of my chastity after last night. I told her I was but maybe not for much longer because I'm going to see Barry again. I told her all the details about last night. She told me she really, really likes Lex but knows he'll be going off to university. I think she should just snog him anyway. He was out tonight and he always talks to her. She also really, really likes Dazza though. She thinks she should pick one but she can't.

Sunday 26th October
The clocks go back today so I get an extra hour of weekend. I feel like I'm wasting it. Nothing seems important any more except going to the pub and Barry.

Monday 27th October
Today I mostly listened to White Zombie and felt restless.

Tuesday 28th October
I stayed up late writing my English coursework and while I was doing that I wasn't thinking about my Dad being dead or about Mum being annoying or all the other niggly stuff in my head. It's really good to focus on something intensely and exclude everything around you for a while. I actually want more English homework.

Wednesday 29th October
Kerrang! is full of Ozzy this week. They've spoiled it with a Bon Jovi poster though. Barry phoned me. Mum was out when he rang so I could talk fairly normally to him. I'm seeing Barry not this Friday but next Friday, which is ages, but he is working a lot and I'm going to a party at Jenni's this Friday. Barry could only meet me on Friday because he's doing overtime and I'm not allowed out late during the week. He said he's looking forward to seeing me again!

Thursday 30th October
I went to HMV with Jenni. She bought My Life With The Thrill Kill Kult's A Crime For All Seasons album.

Friday 31st October

Today is Jenni's favourite day of the year (apart from Christmas, her birthday and Easter). Jenni's parents are letting her have a small Halloween party while they are out at their friend's fiftieth birthday party. Mum said I can stay over at Jenni's, this is brilliant because it means I won't miss any of the party. Jenni invited me, Ian, Lex, Mopey, Dazza, Shot, Ella and Lizzie to her party. She made bat shaped cookies and pizza. Ella suggested we play spin the bottle. Jenni got to kiss Lex! He looked too happy to be a Goth. Dazza looked sort of gloomy. I wonder if they both know that she likes them and both wish the other wasn't there as competition?

November

Saturday 1st November
Mopey Dick was smoking clove cigarettes tonight. The barman came to investigate the weird smell.

Sunday 2nd November
Natalie Imbruglia is at number one with "Torn". Ian thinks she's quite fit. His condoms are still unused. I listened to Suicidal Tendencies' Lights, Camera, Revolution album. The song "Alone" makes me cry. Mrs Butler came round with some magazines for Mum. I read the problem pages. There was; my husband says I'm boring in bed, my boss keeps flirting with me, my colleague keeps taking the credit for my work and men never seem to stay around long after I've slept with them.

Monday 3rd November
Today is the first day of half term. Jenni is doing early Christmas shopping day with her Mum. Ian is playing Doom with Matty. If I wasn't such a resourceful and fascinating individual I'd be bored. I practised dropping my knickers, stepping out of one leg and flicking them up into the air and then catching them. I'm hoping to not be boring in the bedroom, Dear Diary.

Tuesday 4th November
Sometimes when I listen to music it feels like I'm having a holiday in my head and all the bad stuff that buzzes around in it at the moment gets drowned out. I listened to Rancid's ...And Out Come The Wolves three times today.

Ian came round while I was putting the washing away (Mum said I have to help around the house because it's half term). He made me laugh by putting my Wonderbra on and pretending to be a lady. I pinged his bra strap and called him my little cupcake. Then I patted him on the bottom. He giggled and said he wasn't that kind of girl and he didn't want me to get the wrong idea, then he flung himself on my bed and said "Take me! Take me! I can resist no longer". I tickled him until we were both out of breath.

Wednesday 5th November
I went to a bonfire party at Jenni's house. Her Mum asked me yesterday if I wanted to invite Mum, but she was at work. Pam said it must be very hard for us. I wondered what she talking about and then I remembered that Dad was dead. I didn't feel like going to the party but I didn't feel like being on my own either. It was good when I got there. We had sparklers (and wrote rude words with them) and some of Jenni's brother Bruce's friends were there. Bruce is four years older than us but Jenni talks to his friends like they are just normal people. One of them likes prog rock and has long hair. I'll never see him again though because he is at university. Minty came over and told me how sad she was to hear that my Dad had died. I've now got used to hearing this. I've also got used to hearing myself say "It was a terrible shock, thank you for your kind words". Each time I hear it, it gets realer and realer and realer.
Kerrang! wasn't worth buying today. It has Bush on the cover. I bought Terrorizer instead because it's got Motörhead and Venom. I think I'm going to stop buying Kerrang! and get Terroriser instead. Everything dies, including my love of Kerrang!

Thursday 6th November

Jean came round this evening. She wondered if we had seen her and Josie's cat Virginia. She thinks the fireworks startled her last night and she might be hiding somewhere. We looked in our shed, even though it was unlikely and we called out "Ginnie, Ginnie, Ginnie" but no luck. I said I'd keep a look out on my way to school tomorrow because sometimes Ginnie follows me down the street for a bit. Mum came home while we were looking and found the torch so we could look under the big bushes in the garden but still no luck. Mum invited Jean in for coffee and Hob Nobs. If you eat half a packet, are you left with hobs or nobs? Or are the biscuits distributed evenly in the pack so it goes hob, nob, hob, nob etc.?

Friday 7th November

Jean has found Ginnie. She must have come in through the cat flap in the middle of the night. She stopped me on my way to school to tell me and she thanked me for my help. I said "I'm so glad your Ginnie is okay. I always like to stop for a bit of a stroke and a fuss on my way home from school". Mr Moffat from 108 walked past as I was saying this and gave us a very odd look.
I met Barry after he finished work. We went to the pub again. We played table football and had some chips. When I first met him I was too nervous to eat in front of him but I'm not now. He walked me home and we said goodbye at the massive hedge up the road from my house. It took ages to say goodbye. I didn't really want to and he didn't either. I think I could feel his youknowwhat through his trousers. I've actually started being able to talk to him, mainly about music but also about what I'd

like to do after school and gigs I'd like to go to and books I've read.

Saturday 8th November
I love being outside at night. It smells of possibilities and excitement. I saw lots of fireworks on the way to the pub. If there is a heaven my Dad will be getting a great view. If there's not then at least he is in no discomfort or pain. The pub was great. I sat next to T-Reg! He seems so different since he's left school. I felt a bit bad enjoying sitting by him because of Barry. But me and Barry aren't officially boyfriend and girlfriend (yet!!!)
Ian and I walked home together as usual. We paused in the park because he needed a wee. We sat on the bench for a bit and stared at the stars. Ian asked me if Barry ever pressurises me to have sex with him. I said no, he doesn't, but I think he wants to have sex with me (based on his erection). Ian told me to remember that I don't have to do anything I don't want to.

Sunday 9th November
How do you know if a boy is willing to be your boyfriend?
Today I'm mostly listening to Ozzy Osbourne - No More Tears.

Monday 10th November
Bloody Mr Moffat from 108 (excuse my language Dear Diary, but I am fuming) stopped Mum on her way to work to ask her if she thought my chatting unchaperoned to Jean was entirely sensible. He said young minds can be swayed by the exotic. Mum told him that we find Jean and Josie to be wonderful neighbours. He said wasn't she concerned about their proclivities? Mum asked what proclivities and he ummed and ahhed and said they were of a

mind not to marry. Mum said that was none of her concern or his, so long as they didn't have loud parties and they kept their garden tidy. Mum doesn't put up with all of Mr Moffat's nonsense. She isn't homophobic. She doesn't approve of anyone enjoying themselves by having sex.

Mum said she is going to give me more pocket money and a clothing allowance. I've been asking for ages for a clothing allowance, like Jenni gets, but she said she couldn't afford it. Now she is getting a pension from the jewellery company that Dad worked for. Because they were separated and not divorced she is entitled to it. I can't be properly happy about getting what I want because of the reason why I got it.

Tuesday 11th November

"You can spend minutes, hours, days, weeks, or even months over-analysing a situation; trying to put the pieces together, justifying what could've, would've happened... or you can just leave the pieces on the floor and move the fuck on."
— Tupac Shakur

I should note that I'm not usually going to sort out my emotional problems by reference to the works of Tupac. It's just that this particular quote seems useful. It was given to me by Donna Harlow. She doesn't have a Dad either. He's not dead, she just doesn't know who he is. At least I got to know my Dad and had him for fifteen years, some people never even get that. Ian's Mum is still alive but he never sees her. She is not interested in her sons and he lives with that fact every single day. People say nasty things about Donna, they say that she's easy, but I think she is a lovely person, so what if she likes sleeping with boys? If people were honest they would admit that it's only fear of the consequences (or shyness) that stops them from doing what she's doing.

Wednesday 12th November
Janine Sackett did a flamethrower with a bunsen burner and a can of Lynx she nicked out of Mark Dobbs bag in Chemistry today. The supply teacher, Miss Ericson muttered "Dorothy Hodgkin" under her breath and went pale. She confiscated the Lynx and said no one was to turn on a gas tap this lesson because we're doing theory not practice. Our class has seen off a whole load of Chemistry and Physics teachers this year. Baggers is made of stronger stuff and continues chucking Biology our way every week. Some of it even sticks in my head. Janine was dared to do it by Carina Norman. If Carina told her to jump off a bridge she'd probably do it.

Thursday 13th November
I ate some avocado for the first time ever today at Jenni's house. It was quite nice.

Friday 14th November
Yesterday wasn't the first time I've had avocado Dear Diary, it turns out that guacamole is made of avocado. I met Barry and instead of going to the pub we went back to his house because his Mum was out. We snogged on the sofa and he put his hand in my bra! Before he did I told him it was a Wonderbra and then I tried to tell him I was fifteen but he was too busy kissing me to listen! Then he moved pantwards!!! He had a visible stiffy almost all evening!

When I got home I stayed up late watching Airheads because I just couldn't sleep. I was disappointed by Michael McKean, who was David St Hubbins in Spinal Tap, being Milo, a nasty radio station manager and by Judd Nelson*, the hottie from The Breakfast Club being Jimmie Wing, an evil record company executive. Brendan Fraser is very cute but not as cute as Barry. My own hand had to move pantwards before I could get any sleep. I know from the problem pages in Cosmopolitan that this is not a sin and that most women** do this.

*You know what they say about men with big noses, Dear Diary? They need big hankerchiefs!

**Most women who read Cosmopolitan, I'm not sure about the readers of the People's Friend because it doesn't have a sex survey. It does have a story about a group of birds that live in a teapot.

Saturday 15th November
I told Jenni all about what happened with Barry last night then we went to the Green Man. She said I've moved to practice, not theory!

Sunday 16th November
I went to see Nanny Howard. She told me she had been to see a spiritualist and that Dad is safely on the other side and he doesn't want us to grieve for him. He is in a wonderful place and he will see us again in heaven. Dad never believed in God, so it's lovely that God let him go to heaven. But suppose the spiritualist is just telling Nanny what she wants to hear, like the white lies I tell her

(thank you for the jumper, yes Aled Jones is handsome, no, I never have more than one drink).

Monday 17th November
Rubbish day for me today but a great day for Ian. He has got a date! Well, he thinks it's a date. He's going to the cinema on Friday to see Titanic with Natalie West.
I can't stop thinking about what Nanny Howard said and I didn't understand any of Maths today and I burnt my crispy pancakes. Also, do you think you can get pregnant by being fingered? Suppose the fingerer has just had a wank and he hasn't washed his hands and then his sperms get in you? Sorry to be crude, Dear Diary, but this is an issue I need to clarify because my period is late. Also, Dear Diary, I should forewarn you that there are likely to be a lot of adult situations coming up so steel yourself for some mega romps with some hot metal men.
I listened to Slayer's "Spill The Blood" and Entombed's "Blood Song" in the hope that it'll help.

Tuesday 18th November
Yes! I got my period! I celebrated by bouncing on my bed, having a mini mosh pit with Ozzy the bear and Mr Smurf. I was just doing some awesome windmill head banging when Mum came in and asked what all the noise was about. I told her I'd found a pound coin in my knickers drawer. She said it was nice to see me happy and gave me another pound!

Wednesday 19th November
Good things about being fingered:
Practice for actual sex

Might be able to use Tampax in future
Feels nice after a while
Reassurance that you're normal "up there" (would a man mention it if you weren't though?)

Bad things about being fingered:
Where will it lead?
Might get found out
Suppose your period starts at the exact moment you're being fingered?

Miss Ericson surprised us all today by still being our physics teacher. Usually we get through one a week. She overheard Carina tell Janine that Peter Andre is hotter than the sun. She asked Carina how hot the sun is and she didn't know (Carina, not Miss Ericson, obviously she knew or she wouldn't have made a fuss about it, you'd look like a very shit Physics teacher if you didn't know this). Jenni asked did Miss want the temperature of the sun's core or surface? Miss said either. Jenni was the only one who knew. She watches The Sky At Night for fun with her Dad and Bruce.

I didn't buy Kerrang! today. It's all about Metallica's Re-load album. I think I've most definitely grown out of Kerrang! I am now a mature Terrorizer reader. It's still my habit to look at it in WH Smiths but my desire for it is moribund.

Thursday 20th November

The Queen and Prince Philip have been married for fifty years. I wonder what their secret is? Maybe Prince Philip amuses the Queen by putting her bra on and pretending to be a lady. If I was

royalty I could get one of my servants to ask Barry if he wants to be my boyfriend. I could probably get him brought to me, wearing just gold boxer shorts and we could have a freezer full of Viennetta in our bedroom.
Ian asked me and Jenni loads of questions today about what he should do tomorrow when he sees Natalie. They are meeting outside the cinema. He wanted to know if he should pay for her and at what point should he try to snog her? Jenni said Natalie suggested going to the cinema so Ian was under no obligation to pay for her, but if he could afford to then it would be a nice thing to do. I said he'll probably know when she wants to snog him because if she's brave enough to tell him she wants to go to the cinema with him then she's probably brave enough to ask for a snog.

Friday 21st November
I saw Barry tonight. We went back to his house. His Mum goes to bingo every Friday now. I told him I'd got my period and we mainly snogged. He put my hand on the outside of his trousers and I rubbed him! I thought about unzipping him. I told him I was a virgin and I was just about to tell him I was fifteen but we were disturbed by the doorbell. It was some Jehovah's Witnesses. It took ages for them to go. They were quite effective in preventing any sinning unfortunately but I'm sure this is coincidence not divine intervention. If there is a god I'm sure he's got much bigger things to worry about than if I've snuck a look in Barry's pants. We snogged for ages at the massive hedge. I would love to be old enough to have my own place to live and the freedom to do what I want. If Jenni or Ian was dating someone they would be allowed

in their room. Mum gets stroppy about my friendship with Ian so there is no way she'd understand about Barry.

I wonder how Ian's date is going?

Saturday 22nd November
Michael Hutchence of INXS has been found dead in a hotel room. I love the song "Need You Tonight" and the weird names he gave his kids. I feel so sorry for his kids right now. I don't mind being called Cleo even though some people think it's a weird name. It's one thing which my Dad gave me that I will always have. Mum wanted to call me something more common and popular. Jenni told me after he died that I would always have half of his genetic material.
Ian said his date was okayish but the film was truly rubbish, but Natalie thought it was wonderful. He said it was a romantic disaster (the film, not the date). Natalie is quite dull when you actually talk to her at length he said. She isn't very interested in music or computer games. So Natalie West is unlikely to be the girl Ian favours with his first non solo sperm loss mission but Natalie Imbruglia is in with a chance.
Ella told Ian he needs a more mature woman. You didn't need to be Mystic Meg to see that she meant herself.

Sunday 23rd November
I started crying today because we'd run out of Golden Syrup. I used to love sitting on the sofa with Dad eating Golden Syrup on toast. In the winter I'd bring my duvet downstairs and we'd snuggle under it. Sundays are the worst missing Dad days. I'd just about got used to him not living with us and I looked forward to

seeing him every other Sunday. It was starting to feel normal. Mum had even started talking to him a bit and not being quite so arsey after seeing him. During the week I can sort of forget he's dead, but on Sundays there is a massive Dad shaped gap. It's always going to be there.

Monday 24th November
Miss Wallace told me today that there are two wolves fighting inside you. One is evil and is full of anger and lies and unhappiness, one is good and full of joy and beauty and truth and loveliness. The one that wins the fight is the one you feed.
I don't think I need wolves inside me, but I'd be happy if Barry was!

I've just had a Twix. I think the two wolves might have had half each. How do you know which one you are feeding? Why is life so complicated?

Tuesday 25th November
Last night I dreamt that Dad and I were watching telly on the sofa. It was Russ Abbot's Madhouse.
Should I go on the pill? I know I haven't had sex yet but it's bound to happen isn't it? Also, it might make my boobs grow. I could tell Mum I want it to make my periods better. I've been reading about it in one of Mrs Butler's magazines.

Wednesday 26th November
It's Jenni's birthday on Friday so me and Ian went shopping for presents for her. He bought her a book: I, Strahd: The Memoirs of a Vampire by P. N. Elrod. I got her a sew it yourself furry bat kit in

Jacksons haberdashery department that she always looks at and some purple and black striped tights from Heelas.

Kerrang! this week is just full of Steven Tyler being sleazy so I wasn't going to buy it but it's got next year's year planner in so I bought it. Next year has to be better than this year. Being sixteen is going to be a huge relief. I feel like an adult trapped in the age of a child.

Thursday 27th November
I had quinoa at Jenni's but you say it "keen-waah", how confusing is that? It sounds like a martial art or an exotic bird that David Attenborough might creep up on. It's a very fancy name for something which doesn't taste of much. We listened to Jack Off Jill's Sexless Demons and Scars album and wrote our Gods lists.

My Gods list (international)
Pete Steele
Glenn Danzig
Christopher Lee
Rob Zombie
Max Cavalera
Rob Newman
Lars Frederiksen
Dave Mustaine
Dave Lister
Elvira Mistress Of The Dark

My Gods list (Reading)
Barry
Tyrannosaurus Reg

Jenni's Gods list (international)
Pete Steele
Robert Smith
Trent Reznor
Marilyn Manson
Jessicka (from Jack Off Jill)
Twiggy Ramirez
Johnny Depp
Kat Bjelland
Tommy Lee
Kiefer Sutherland

Jenni's Gods list (Reading)
Lex
Darren

Friday 28th November
When my underwear started commenting on the wildlife, I realised I had accidentally bought a David Attenbra!
I wrote this joke myself, Dear Diary. If Russ Abbot was still on telly I'd send it to him as an idea for a sketch.
Today is Jenni's sixteenth birthday so Ian and I went round for dinner. Her brother Bruce and his girlfriend Minty were also there. We had spinach and ricotta cannelloni (Jenni's current favourite) and chocolate fudge cake for dessert. Jenni is now old enough to buy cigarettes, get married and have sex. She could go on the pill without her parents being told. Famous people who share her birthday are Martin Clunes from Men Behaving Badly, Judd Nelson from The Breakfast Club and Anna Nicole Smith

(always in the Daily Mail because she once married a really old man probably for money but she said she loved him).
Mum bought me a Barbie advent calendar. It's more pink than it is Christmassy.

Saturday 29th November
We went to the Green Man to celebrate Jenni's birthday. Usually we just go to celebrate Saturday.

Sunday 30th November
How do people know which sex noises to make when? Should I try Tampax?

December

Monday 1st December
Today I'm mostly trying not to feel sad. Dad loved Christmas, but he isn't here to enjoy it now. Ian and Gav have got Sonic The Hedgehog advent calendars. Jenni has got a fair trade one from Oxfam. Carina Norman overheard us talking about this and tried to embarrass Jenni, saying "Yeah, I've seen your Mum shopping in Oxfam" but Jenni told her they do good coffee and they help the disadvantaged and just wasn't embarrassed so Carina gave up. In Maths Matty Bateman farted and it sounded exactly like the start of the theme tune to Jonny Briggs.
I spent the evening reading the Woolies Winter Wonderland catalogue. The toys just seem like gaudy trinkets to me now, Dear Diary. I still read it from cover to cover though.

Tuesday 2nd December
I need to stop worrying about people I love dying. I've become preoccupied with this thought, wondering who will be next. I need to remember Lady Macbeth's "let things without all remedy be without regard", although there sort of is a remedy for heart disease if it is caught in time. If Dad had still lived here with me and Mum, instead of on his own, would he still be alive? This thought keeps going round in my head. I need to find some way of exorcising it.

Wednesday 3rd December
The last will and testament of Cleo Howard:
I leave my music to Ian Edwards and my clothes to Jenni Maxwell. I leave my books to the school library. I leave my heart to Barry

(figuratively, but I also leave it literally to be transplanted into someone else or if it's knackered genetically like Dad's was, then to medical research).
I've been listening to Paradise Lost's Gothic album all evening. I told Mum I needed money for STs but actually I'm going to buy Tampax.

Thursday 4th December
I bought Tampax today and a box of Walnut Whips for Mum for Christmas. If you squint the blue boxes look similar. I'm trying to think of an album or T-shirt to buy Barry for Christmas.

Friday 5th December
Brilliant day! I saw Barry today and he said he really missed me when he didn't see me last week (I was at Jenni's birthday dinner). I said I missed him too. This has been the best day for ages and the first time I haven't thought about Dad loads since he died. Barry's Mum was at bingo as usual so we went to his house. He asked me if I wanted to go upstairs and said we didn't have to and he wouldn't do anything I didn't want to. We lay on his bed and kissed for ages. It was one of the best snogs I've ever had in my life. He had his hands on the back of my neck while his tongue was in my mouth and it was the kind of kiss that leaves your knickers moist. Even when I got home I couldn't stop thinking about it. I kept trying to tell him I was fifteen but most of the time his tongue was in my mouth.

Saturday 6th December
We went to Poundland and Jenni got some purple sparkly wool. She is going to learn to knit. She has already made the bat from

the kit I bought her for her birthday and hung it from her ceiling. We went to Graffiti in Smelly Alley and I got some Stargazer glitter nail varnish and some matching glitter make up that you can use as eye shadow or blusher. It's sort of all the colours at once, depending on where the light hits the glitter. I love going round the shops at Christmas. We spent ages looking at the decorations in Heelas and Jacksons.

I wore my Alice Cooper T-shirt, snake print skirt and red studded belt to the Green Man tonight and had a glittery face and glittery nails. Glitter makes me feel cheerful. I think I'll wear it all December.

Lex told me my nail varnish is iridescent. Other things that can be iridescent are soap bubbles and butterfly wings. Shot said I remind her of a sweet little fairy. This is one of the loveliest things anyone has ever said to me.

Sunday 7th December

The Teletubbies are number one. What is wrong with this country? We used to have a reputation for making great music. I like the bit at the start of the Teletubbies where some bunnies are quietly hopping about and nibbling grass but then their habitat is ruined by some brightly coloured morons appearing and running about the place.

Monday 8th December

Carina Norman wants the Peter Andre album for Christmas. If I was Santa she would be getting coal but since life is unfair she'll probably get what she wants.

Tuesday 9th December
Mr Freeman told us today that the French Father Christmas has got a helper called Père Fouettard that spanks the bad French children. Having never been to France, and not knowing any actual French people, I'm never sure if the things Mr Freeman tells us are true or if he's just making stuff up to fill time before the bell goes. He also told us that the people of Lyon put candles in their window to celebrate the Virgin Mary. I feel sorry for Mary. It must have been embarrassing that everyone knew she was a virgin plus she didn't even have sex and she had to give birth, which is grim. I'd be embarrassed if even my class knew my sexual history (I know I don't actually have one yet, but I'm hoping to get one soon. I wonder if Père Fouettard would consider this intention a spankable offence or whether he's more relaxed about it because he's French? Jenni went topless in France but it was apparently normal so it's clearly not as uptight as Reading).

Wednesday 10th December
I'm reading Hogfather by Terry Pratchett again. Right now I feel safer and happier in Discworld than in this world. Some days Dear Diary, I feel okay, some days I feel okay and then I feel guilty that I feel okay when Dad is dead and other days I feel bleak and sad right from the minute I wake up.

Thursday 11th December
Mum asked me if there is anything I'd like as a treat because she knows I've had a hard time lately. I said there was a black lace dress in Dorothy Perkins I'd like. She said she'll give me the

money and I can go and get it tomorrow. I made us both a cup of tea.

Friday 12th December
I got my dress after work. I love it. I think Barry does too. Unfortunately I also got my period. I bled in my new knickers which was annoying. Damn my unreliable fanny. Me and Barry went to his house and lay on his bed. I put my hand inside his trousers!! I know what I want for Christmas Dear Diary! It is not available in the Woolie's Winter Wonderland catalogue!

Saturday 13th December
Ella came out with mistletoe tonight. She kissed most of the pub. She has got some balls. Lizzie suggested she focus on the two or three men she actually fancies and then Ella got in a bit of a huff. Lizzie and Ella have been friends since junior school. Ella is much more man hungry than Lizzie is.
When we were walking home Ian said he would be scared of Ella comparing him to other men if he had sex with her.

Sunday 14th December
Mum is very grumpy today. I offered to paint her nails glittery (this cheers me up, Dear Diary) but she said she is not allowed fancy nails at work. I need to make sure I get a job where I'm allowed to wear what I want.

Monday 15th December
Something is bothering me a lot Dear Diary. Barry still thinks I'm in the sixth form. I never told him I was, he just thought I was and I didn't tell him I wasn't. This was ages ago, before we were

spending time together alone. It seems wrong not to tell him, I probably should have mentioned it ages before and I do keep trying but sometimes when we're together it just doesn't seem important. We don't talk about school or his work much because it's boring. I do keep trying to tell him but not finding the right moment.

Mr Kennedy gave us loads of Maths homework. For the love of Lemmy, doesn't he have any Christmas spirit? I wouldn't mind if he regularly gave us homework but he doesn't that often.

Tuesday 16th December
I asked Jenni if she thought I should tell Barry I'm not in the sixth form. She said I should and was surprised I hadn't already. It's alright for her, she's good at talking to people and she is already sixteen so doesn't have to worry about this. If she was going out with Barry she would probably just tell him she was going to have sex with him in about six months and then offer him some couscous while he waits (which he'd be allowed to eat in her bedroom). Suppose I tell Barry and he's angry with me for not telling him before? Some men don't seem to care about how old you are. Barry is a bright spot in my dark existence, a warm body in a cold, lonely world.

I asked Ian what he thought and he said it's okay when people who are both underage have sex if they are mature enough, but not if it's people of different ages, especially if one of them doesn't know the true age of the other one. I know he's right.

Mrs Butler came round with some magazines for Mum so I read the problem pages. There was a lot of stuff about people's families being awkward at Christmas. I don't have the dilemma of

which of my parents to spend Christmas with now I only have one.
I'm going to tell Barry I'm almost sixteen as soon as I see him on Friday.

Wednesday 17th December

Ian and I went to see Betty after school. Ian got the Christmas tree and decorations out of the loft for her. Betty said she was getting too old to go up there. She said she tries not to moan about getting old because there are many people who aren't lucky enough to get old. She let us eat some of the chocolate tree decorations. We made some snowflakes out of folded paper to stick on Betty's kitchen window because the ones Ian and Gav made years ago have got ripped.

Thursday 18th December

I visited Nanny Howard today and she told me to go and take anything I wanted from Dad's old wardrobe. I stood inside it for a while and I couldn't help crying at the smell of him. It was so real but he is so dead. I made myself stop crying because I didn't want to upset Nanny. I already feel bad that I leave it ages between visits. I took a couple of rugby shirts and I found condoms in a jacket pocket of Dads! It was a full packet of eighteen with none of them used. This could mean one of two things:
1. My Dad was a very optimistic man, who didn't get laid (like father, like daughter!)
2. My Dad was such a prolific shagger he had to buy condoms in large size packs (I have no evidence of him ever having relations with anyone except Mum)

Or, there was a special offer on in Boots. He did always like a bargain.

I've taken them to literally protect Nanny from finding protection. They were Durex featherlite. I never expected to find out my Dad's preferred condom brand. I'm hiding them inside my Holly Hobbie night dress case. I never wear a night dress anyway, just a Slayer T-shirt.

Friday 19th December

Well I'll never be needing condoms. I met Barry tonight and on the walk to his house I told him that I wasn't in the sixth form. He wasn't angry exactly but he was weird with me. He said we were still mates and that he'll say hello when he sees me in the Green Man but he doesn't want to take me back to his house when his Mum is out and he can't see me this Friday because he's got to visit family for Christmas. He said maybe he would take me for a drink again next year but he might not. I pretended I understood but I don't really. I came home and cried for ages and when Mum came in from work she thought I was crying about Dad and she said she knows how I feel and she misses him too. Then I started crying about Dad and Barry. I feel like everyone leaves me. Then I started crying because Mum says she knows how I feel, but actually she doesn't, she has no idea of the things that are really, truly important to me. I let Mum hug me for a bit.

Saturday 20th December

Condom questions:

What would I have thought if they had been fruit flavour?
What would I have thought if the pack had been half empty?
What would have happened last night if I hadn't told Barry?

Mum asked me if I'm going to put the Christmas decorations up this weekend. I suppose I should. I went into town and bought Rammstein's Sehnsucht album for Jenni and a Red Dwarf T-shirt with Lister on for Ian. My Christmas shopping is now done. Every one of the magazines Mrs Butler brought round has a slightly different mince pie recipe and Mum was deciding which ones to make. She asked me what I thought of puff pastry and said she thinks filo is a step too far.

I went to the pub and left Mum with her pastry quandary. It really doesn't matter to me. Ella sat on the lap of a cute guy in a Santa hat tonight. He looked about thirty! She had mistletoe with her again. T-Reg tucked it into his belt and asked her to kiss him under it! Mopey Dick called him unoriginal but Dear Diary, I suspect he'd have tucked mistletoe into his belt quick as a flash if it would get him a kiss from Ella. He is about the only one who hasn't had at least a snog from her. She told me she doesn't like people who think they are superior to other people. Mopey isn't bad looking but he seems mean and bitchy sometimes. When we were leaving the pub everyone hugged everyone because it's Christmas. I got to smell T-Reg up close.

Sunday 21st December
This morning the front page of the Reading Chronicle didn't read "Mince Pie Pastry Change Creates Hole in Space-time Continuum".
I can't stop listening to The Ramones' Too Tough To Die album.

Monday 22nd December
Mum is working overtime so Ian came round. I started putting up the Christmas decorations and he helped. Then I started crying

and he hugged me for ages and said it was okay and that he'll always be there for me. He gave me a tissue when I stopped crying and he carried on hugging me and I felt a bit weird. I could hear his heart beating and he smelt good (he doesn't wear aftershave like T-Reg, he wears Lynx Oriental). He was stroking my hair and telling me not to be sad because my Dad wouldn't want me to be sad. Then he had to go because Mum was coming home.

Tuesday 23rd December
I went to see Nanny Howard this morning. I invited Mum but she didn't want to come. She said she was knackered from work. I took Nanny a box of New Berry Fruits and a Christmas card from me and Mum. Nanny is going to Uncle Brian's for Christmas. She asked me how school was and if I was courting. I didn't say much, I'm still gutted about the Barry situation and clueless as to how to start a T-Reg situation. Nanny said I used to never stop talking and now I don't say boo to a goose. She gave me some money for Christmas. She said she always used to get Dad to buy my present so she didn't get it wrong.
I went to Ian's after seeing Nanny. I feel all wrong today, like I'm a bad person and that's why my life is going wrong. Ian told me I'm a triple fried egg, chili, chutney sandwich. He told me all my ingredients may be odd (cheers Mate!) but I'm great. He said he knew how to fix me. He made me a cup of hot chocolate and gave me a Spira to suck it up with. It's a new invention of Gav's and it is brilliant.

Wednesday 24th December
Ian and I went round to Jenni's today. Her house looks lovely at Christmas. There was a holly wreath on the door and they have a real Christmas tree. Ian and I sniffed it. We both have a plastic one at home. When I got home Mum and I watched telly together for a bit (we don't usually do this because she likes rubbish). We watched the Two Fat Ladies cooking programme Christmas special. They went to a posh school and cooked a Christmas pudding ice cream bombe which looked lush. Then Mum touched the stair carpet for luck before we watched the lottery results (but Mum hadn't won).

Thursday 25th December
I got a bass guitar! It's second hand but that's okay because it's probably been played by some amazing musicians. Mum cooked dinner and we took it round to Nanny Brooks and warmed it up in the microwave. She didn't know it was Christmas day, despite the sheltered accommodation being decorated and having the telly on and watching Noel's Christmas Presents. Mum acted all jolly and we pulled crackers and wore our paper hats. Mine kept sliding into my eyes while Mum and Nanny's stayed perched on their permed hair.
Mum told me on the way home that she worries that her memory will go like Nanny's has. Even though today is Christmas day it wasn't all that wonderful. Mum usually pretends things are fine but today she actually said that the first Christmas without Dad is bound to be a difficult one.
We bumped into Josie on our way home and she invited us in for some mulled wine and mince pies. We went in and joined the party. It was all ladies but still fun. I liked the mulled wine but

Mum made us go home after one drink. There was a woman there who looked a bit like Shot but older. I was telling her about heavy metal and she sounded interested.

Friday 26th December
My bass guitar is disappointing. Mum didn't realise I also need an amp to go with it. I'm going to ask for one for my birthday or save up for one. Also everything I want to play hurts my fingers because it's at the top end where the strings are thickest. I have one book of bass tab called the Bass Tab White Pages, it has loads of songs, but most of them are pop songs. I had a bash at Judas Priest's "Living After Midnight".

Saturday 27th December
The Green Man was phenomenal last night. Everyone was out because everyone got money for Christmas. T-Reg was drunk. Now he's working he's got more money to spend and he's investing some of it in lager he says. He bought me a Malibu and Diet Coke. Then he told me how he'd like to do it to me! No-one else was listening. Jenni was talking to Lex and Ian was talking to Bob and STF. T-Reg said he'd start off slow because he knows I haven't done it before and he'd tell me to brace myself and then he'd do it to me until I liked it. I didn't say anything, I just blushed. He also said he'd have a wank beforehand so that he didn't jizz too quickly. He sounds so considerate Dear Diary, I think he's a gentleman, what do you think?
Ian also got a guitar for Christmas and an amp. Jenni got some New Rock boots.

Sunday 28th December

Would a sober T-Reg like to do it to me? Will he remember what he said last night when I see him next? Also, you can brace yourself, but can you brace other people?

Today I mostly ate selection box. Unfortunately it had the Spice Girls on the front. It was a gift from Aunty Alice, along with the Spice Girls annual. Aunty Alice thinks all teenagers like the same things. Is there nowhere the Spice Girls haven't colonised? I expect to see them when I lift the lid of the loo, or open my underwear drawer. They are abso-bloody-lutely all over the place. Apart from the Spice Girls taint it was a very good selection box. The inside contained a Wispa Gold, a Fuse, a Crunchie, a Curly Wurly, a Fudge, a Boost, a Caramel and Chocolate Buttons. I still miss Barry. I'd even give him my Wispa Gold. However maybe it's T-Reg who is meant to be my first proper serious love?

Monday 29th December

What do you call a difficult to hear Iron Maiden album? Mumbler of the beast!
What did Bruce Dickinson say to Steve Harris when they were trapped inside a fish? Run for the gills!
Who is the grumpiest member of Judas Priest? K. K. Frowning!
If I made Christmas crackers these are the jokes I'd put in them (and elephant jokes). I'd make the crackers black and silver and they would have mini bottles of Malibu in them and Alice Cooper badges.
Ian came round and changed the action on my bass so it hurts my fingers less. He said we could start a band if I want.

Tuesday 30th December
I went to the cinema with Jenni and Minty to see George Of The Jungle. It was basically only watchable because of beautiful Brendan Fraser in a loin cloth for the first half of the film.

Wednesday 31st December
I watched the final of World's Strongest Man today. I'm going to do something to make my Dad proud of me. I don't know what it is yet. I'm going to try to be kinder to Mum (apart from when she tries to tell me what to wear) and make her cups of tea more often and not leave plates and mugs in my room. I'm going to go and see Nanny Howard more often, even if she does say mad stuff about messages from Dad in heaven. I'm going to make 1998 the year I get some action. I'm going to listen to Zodiac Mindwarp's Cleopatra Rising every morning. I'm going to stop being shy, I'm going to grab life by the balls.

List of Characters in Cleo's Diary

Jenni Maxwell – Self-assured posh Goth Jenni always knows what she wants and this means she always gets it. Best friends with Cleo and Ian. She's aiming for a career in science. She has dyed black hair, is five feet and nine inches tall.

Ian Edwards - Best friends with Cleo and Jenni. He is geeky enough to be interesting but not geeky enough to be weird. Sometimes good guys don't wear white and he is almost always wearing a black T-shirt. He's slim, almost six feet tall, and has long, straight, very dark brown hair past his shoulders. He doesn't know quite how handsome he is.

Margaret "Peggy" Howard - Mum of Cleo. She's an undiagnosed sufferer of depression and retreater from life since her marriage break-up. She's trying her best and she stays within her routines to keep herself functioning. She sometimes can't believe she gave birth to Cleo. They are very different people who would like to get along but sometimes struggle to understand each other's point of view.

Charles "Chas" Howard – Cleo's Dad. He got married young to Cleo's Mum. He used to be the assistant manager of a shoe shop and is now the assistant manager of a jewellers shop. He was smart enough for university but he didn't go. Grandad Howard and Nanny Howard couldn't see the point in it.

Susan "Nanny" Brooks - Peggy's Mum, Cleo's Grandmother. Nanny Brooks has dementia and lives in sheltered accommodation.

Lily "Nanny" Howard – Mum of Chas Howard, Grandmother of Cleo Howard. She is an avid watcher of both Emmerdale and Coronation Street, an expert trifle maker and a good knitter.

Mrs Winifred Butler – Neighbour and regular bringer rounder of women's magazines and occasional bringer rounder of well-meant but dreaded marrows. She is very proud of her rose bushes.

Barry Maynard – A long haired and attractive builder who likes metal. He is very hairy and has a single eyebrow (much like Bert from Sesame Street).

Betty Edwards - Beloved Mum of Terry and Nan of Ian and Gavin. Proud displayer of family photos, fond of chocolate oranges at Christmas, always got a full biscuit tin. Thinks Cleo would be the perfect girlfriend for Ian.

Terry Edwards - Dad of Ian and Gavin, son of Betty. He was deserted by his wife who ran off with another man. What hurts Terry the most is that she doesn't bother keeping in contact with Ian and Gavin. Terry firmly believes that Elvis is alive and well and faked his own death because he got tired of his celebrity lifestyle.

Pam Maxwell - Jenni's Mum. A partial feminist who wishes her daughter would wear slightly less weird clothes.

Roy Maxwell - Jenni's Dad, Sociology lecturer and feminist. He is pleased that his daughter chooses to wear weird clothes. Roy is a very liberal parent who believes he needs to give his children the skills to make their own decisions.

Bruce Maxwell – Older brother of Jenni Maxwell by four years. Bruce is an undergraduate, studying anthropology.

Gavin Edwards – The older brother of Ian by five years, son of Terry and grandson of Betty. Gav lives and works in Reading but feels he's growing out of it. He and Ian are firm friends as well as siblings.

Alf Edwards - Husband of Betty, father of Terry, Grandad of Ian and Gav.

Jean Peters – Lesbian (not Welsh) neighbour. She lives at number ninety-six and has a cat called Virginia (known as Ginnie).

Josie Ashton – Lesbian (not Goth or metal head) neighbour. She lives at number ninety-six and has a cat called Virginia (known as Ginnie).

Mr Moffat – A grumpy neighbour who lives at number one hundred and eight. He's very active in the neighbourhood watch.

Araminta "Minty" Jarvis – The girlfriend of Bruce's Maxwell. She wears white trousers and is jolly. She's studying Meteorology.

Teachers

Mr Murray – The headmaster at Ian, Cleo and Jenni's comprehensive school. Brown of suit and tired of mind. He would prefer you not to wear a rude T-shirt.

Miss Wallace – The woman responsible for teaching English to Cleo, Jenni and Ian at school. Kind hearted and out of her depth when it comes to class control.

Mr "Baggers" Bagnell – Biology teacher. Wears brown tweed trousers and pink shirts with big pointy collars and is a bit pervy.

Mr Kennedy – Maths teacher. He wears shirts with little squares on that look like graph paper. He doesn't much enjoy teaching Maths.

Mr "Weebles" Webbley – German teacher. He has only been to Germany twice but enjoyed it hugely both times due to German beer.

Mr Venables – Physics teacher. He finds that when you've considered the mysteries of other universes and of the creation of the world, whether or not a group of fifteen year olds listens to you or not is unimportant.

Miss Ericson - Chemistry supply teacher. She's pluckier than the average supply teacher and an admirer of Margaret Thatcher.

Mrs Nicholson – The school secretary. She's always calm, having dealt with many emergencies over the years. She takes two custard creams and a cup of coffee to Mr Murray at eleven every day. Every day he watches her bottom retreat in a tight skirt and he thinks a thought that would shock the children whose education he is responsible for. Mrs Nicholson senses this and walks slowly to the door.

Mrs Savage - Textiles teacher. Is easily embarrassed and is happiest when showing some of the keen girls how to cut patterns or do buttonholes.

Mrs Rogers – Humanities teacher. She used to teach just Religious Education but now has to teach humanities as well. She has read Aldous Huxley's Brave New World and she doesn't like it.

Miss Douglas – P.E. teacher. She is sick of being asked every year if it's true that too much P.E. makes you a lesbian. She schedules swimming knowing full well it will result in forged excuse notes but knows you can lead a teenage girl to the sports centre but the law forbids you from making them swim.

Mr Askew – CDT teacher. He is nearing retirement and he preferred teaching when it was woodwork for the boys and sewing for the girls.

Mr Freeman - French teacher. He is one of the youngest teachers at the school. He thinks he's cool.

Year 10/Lower fifth – Cleo's school year

Natalie West – One of the cutest girls in Cleo's school year. Ian is enamoured of her but with no real expectation of getting anywhere.

Mark Dobbs – The class pervert. If a copy of Razzle is found on school premises, it's highly likely you can trace it back to him. He often wears T-shirts handed down to him by his older brother, some of which are not the most appropriate school wear.

Donna Harlow – Sits next to Cleo often due to having a surname beginning with H. She likes rap music and hip hop. Her hair is styled in a brown bob, like Posh Spice. This is a very common hairstyle.

Charmaine Payne – A class mate who has a huge crush on Ian. Her mild flirtations never hit home.

Carina Norman – The class bitch. The rain on many people's parades, the wasp in the apple, the headache in the whisky, every school has one. Take a minute to boo and hiss if you can remember the individual at your school who fitted this role.

Janine Sackett – The shadow and sidekick of Carina Norman. A weak individual, she assists in Carina's mission to suck the fun out of school for as many persons as possible.

Matthew "Matty" Bateman – Good mate of Ian's and fellow computer game enthusiast. Matty is often in the same lessons as Ian, Cleo and Jenni. He makes no attempt to hide his flatulence.

Sally Walker – In the same school year as Cleo but is not in many of the same lessons. She wears make up most of the time and occasionally wears a Guns N' Roses T-shirt. Cleo can't quite work out if she's a full on metal fan or if she just likes a bit of soft rock.

Mark Price – His only part in this tale is dragging Donna Harlow into the boy's toilets where she claims she saw Dave Chamber's willy.

Dave Chambers – His only part in this tale is that Donna Harlow claimed she saw his part when Mark Price dragged her into the boy's toilets. He insists she can only have seen his bum.

Year 11/Upper fifth – The school year above Cleo
Owen Tranter – The hardest kid in the school. He is friendly with T-Reg so leaves the metal kids alone mostly.

Reg "Tyrannosaurus" "T-Reg" Atherton – He was named Reginald after his Grandad. He gets called Tyrannosaurus because Reg is such an old fashioned name. He's a metal head, an over user of aftershave and the grower of a reluctant moustache. Cleo is always pleased to see and smell him.

Death Metal Darren "Dazza" Baskerville – A metal head who Jenni finds dazzling. He has lots of black hair. His favourite bands are Cannibal Corpse and Immortal.

Simon "The Raspberry" Duffy aka STR – A metal head. He is named because he spits a tiny bit when he speaks and when he was overexcited once he made a raspberry noise. Another candidate nickname was Yosemite Sam but this was felt to be a huge exaggeration of his mainly minor idiosyncratic speech. Roy Hattersley was also briefly considered as a nickname (due to the literally spitting Spitting Image puppet) but again this was over egging it.

Bob Hawkins – A metal head whose party trick is fellating bananas. He has actually had sex, unlike most of his contemporaries who talk a big game but have had very little real life experience.

Daniella "Ella" Barclay – She likes soft rock, hard rock and some metal, nothing heavier than Metallica. She has an impressive chest and she worries about her weight. She has her hair in a shaggy perm, like David Coverdale. She gets around a bit and likes to practice on boys in her year. She'd like to be Pamela Anderson when she grows up.

Elisabeth "Lizzie" Snowden - Lizzie is a big Bon Jovi fan and a huge Kiss fan. She's often a reluctant double dater with Ella. She's slow to see the charms of the boys around her.

Sadie "Shot" Gunn - A punk goddess who Cleo looks up to, both literally and figuratively. Shot is the only punk in the school. She's kind, opinionated and Cleo is perhaps a little bit in love with her.

Jessica Rice – She dates Owen Tranter even though he bit her on the bottom. In later years Jessica will develop some interesting bedroom preferences.

Year 12/Sixth form first years
Alexander "Lex" Frost – He's Goth and gorgeous. Jenni talks to him at every opportunity.

"Mopey" Dick Rippingdale – He is an assiduous Goth and he tends towards the pretentious. He is just as likely to be moronic as Byronic.

About The Author

Photo by Bernie Galewski

Sarah Tipper was born in Oxford in 1974 and was very nearly called Robert. She enjoyed school, especially any classes that involved writing and that did not involve wearing shorts. She once sniggered her way through an entire assignment about the Cerne Abbas giant. At age thirteen Sarah started listening to metal. She was lightly teased for wearing tight jeans and an Anthrax or Slayer T-shirt. This didn't bother her, she felt safe from the Bros dross culture other teenagers at the time were so keen on. Sarah's religion is heavy metal. Her favourite biscuit is the chocolate shortcake ring. The best gigs she's ever been to were Suicidal Tendencies, Manowar, Dedlok and Bolt-Thrower. She can't cope with the responsibility of having a pet but if she could she'd have a ginger rabbit called Ronnie (after Ronnie James Dio).

    Sarah studied Psychology at the University of Reading. She missed her graduation ceremony because it clashed with seeing Black Sabbath. She went on to graduate with a Masters in Health Psychology from Coventry University. Luckily this didn't clash with anything and her Mum got a nice day out.

During the day Sarah does cancer research, squirting things at other things in a science type way. She started writing her first novel because a friend kept telling her to write a book and because another friend had inspired her to write a "things to do before you're forty list" and write a book made it on to this list.

The idea of the Eviscerated Panda trilogy (A Metal Tale, Back In Bamboo and Vulgar Display Of Panda) was conceived after twenty-four years of experience of going to gigs and drinking in rock pubs and twenty-five years of experience of listening to metal. It was hugely enjoyable to write and Sarah hopes to create heavymetalworld, much like Terry Pratchett created Discworld. Writing The Very Metal Diary Of Cleo Howard involved drinking Malibu for research purposes and the purchase of a Viennetta (which seems to have become less ornate since the nineties, although Sarah worries that maybe she's become too sophisticated to see the beauty of it). The author photo was taken by the lovely Bernie Galewski during a strange evening that involved giant pencils and a glittery skull.